The sound of a throat being loudly cleared filled the uneasy silence.

Hannah closed her eyes. Just what she'd hoped to avoid—a witness to her family's dysfunction and her personal humiliation.

She opened her eyes and turned to face her customer. *Russell Danielson.* She'd met Russell this past summer. They'd hit it off and spent a glorious evening together. He'd promised to contact her when he got back to his duty station. He hadn't.

She'd been hurt when he'd ghosted her— disappointed, even—but not surprised.

Russell looked around the room, taking in the scene, and then smiled. "Sorry I'm late."

"Uh." Late for what? Until he'd stepped into her store, she hadn't known he was in town.

He crossed the room, not stopping until he was standing an inch in front of her. Before she could utter a word, he put his arms around her waist and pulled her into a kiss. He lingered for a few seconds before pulling away.

"Who are you?" Hannah's ex demanded.

Russell spun around slowly, drawing himself up to his full height. "I'm Russell Danielson. Hannah and I are dating."

They were? That was news to her.

* * *

SWEET BRIAR SWEETHEARTS:
There's something about Sweet Briar...

Dear Reader,

Christmas. It's the most wonderful time of the year.

I love the lights and songs and the excitement that fills the air. I especially love Christmas romances and I've longed to write one of my own. *A Soldier Under Her Tree* is my first Christmas book, although I hope it's not my last.

This book tells the story of newly minted Scrooge, boutique owner Hannah Carpenter, who can't wait for the season to end, and soldier Russell Danielson, who makes it his mission to restore her Christmas spirit.

Thank you so much for picking up *A Soldier Under Her Tree*. I hope you enjoy it.

I love hearing from my readers. Please feel free to visit my website, kathydouglassbooks.com, and drop me a line. While you're there, sign up for my newsletter. You can also find me on Facebook, Instagram and Twitter.

Happy reading!

Kathy

A Soldier Under Her Tree

KATHY DOUGLASS

HARLEQUIN
SPECIAL
EDITION

HARLEQUIN®
SPECIAL
EDITION™

Recycling programs
for this product may
not exist in your area.

ISBN-13: 978-1-335-89499-1

A Soldier Under Her Tree

Copyright © 2020 by Kathleen Gregory

For questions and comments about the quality of this book,
please contact us at CustomerService@Harlequin.com.

Harlequin Enterprises ULC
22 Adelaide St. West, 40th Floor
Toronto, Ontario M5H 4E3, Canada
www.Harlequin.com

Printed in U.S.A.

Kathy Douglass came by her love of reading naturally—both of her parents were readers. She would finish one book and pick up another. Then she attended law school and traded romances for legal opinions.

After the birth of her two children, her love of reading turned into a love of writing. Kathy now spends her days writing the small-town contemporary novels she enjoys reading.

Books by Kathy Douglass

Harlequin Special Edition

Sweet Briar Sweethearts

How to Steal the Lawman's Heart
The Waitress's Secret
The Rancher and the City Girl
Winning Charlotte Back
The Rancher's Return
A Baby Between Friends
The Single Mom's Second Chance
A Soldier Under Her Tree

Furever Yours

The City Girl's Homecoming

Montana Mavericks: What Happened to Beatrix?

The Maverick's Baby Arrangement

Visit the Author Profile page
at Harlequin.com for more titles.

To my readers.
I am so grateful for you. Whether you've read each of my books, some of them or this is the first that you've picked up, I appreciate your support.

To Charles Griemsman.
You are an extraordinary editor. Your insightful comments help me turn ordinary characters into real people. We make a great team.

To my husband and sons.
Thank you so much for your consistent love and support. I love you all with my whole heart.

Chapter One

Hannah Carpenter muttered to herself as she dragged the ladder toward the string of unlit Christmas lights, hoping against hope that she'd find the burned-out one on the first try. Not that she expected it to be easy. There were at least forty lights that were no longer blinking on this display near the jewelry rack. She didn't have time to waste on this nonsense. If she had her druthers, she'd pull down all of the decorations, shove them into a box and forget that Christmas even existed.

But she couldn't. Christmas season had a big impact on her boutique's annual bottom line. The sales from the day after Thanksgiving to Christmas Eve were nearly double those from January through March. Since she had bills to pay and employees depending on her for their livelihood, she'd leave the lights on and keep blasting the Christmas music, setting the mood for those customers who enjoyed the season. She might not possess the holiday spirit, but she knew how to keep up appearances.

She yanked out a bulb. No change, so she put it back and tried the one beside it.

She hadn't always been a scrooge. Christmastime used to be her favorite season. She'd even planned her wedding for December 22. But that was before she'd caught her ex-fiancé in bed with her sister a week before the big day. Gerald's initial shock and lame apologies had quickly morphed into indignation that she'd shown up at his place unannounced. To Hannah's disbelief, Dinah had only smirked and tucked the blankets around her body more securely as if Hannah had been the interloper. Yeah, that experience three years ago had killed her love of Christmas and all of its associated gaiety.

Even now, Hannah could picture her sister's grin, and her stomach began to churn. Hannah forced the unhappy memory away as she yanked out another light. In thirty-three years she hadn't been able to figure out what motivated her sister to act the way she did. She doubted today would be the day it all became clear. And did it really matter? Her sister was no longer a part of her life.

After that heartbreak, Hannah had quit her job where she'd worked with Gerald, and moved from Virginia to Sweet Briar, North Carolina. Shortly thereafter, she'd opened her boutique, Designs by Hannah. It had taken a lot of work and even more good luck, but her boutique was successful. More important, she'd made a happy life for herself.

After twenty-five tries, Hannah found the defective bulb, replaced it with the spare, descended the ladder and returned it to the storeroom. When she went back to the front of the shop, she looked around, checking to be sure that everything was in order. Every blouse, scarf, skirt and dress was hanging perfectly from its respective rack. There wasn't a speck of dust on her gleaming oak floors, and the gold-trimmed mirrors were spotless. She'd changed the window display from the typical mannequins dressed in one of her outfits to three elves placing neatly folded blouses wrapped in ribbon under a decorated tree. Every day kids pressed their fingers and noses on the window while they stared at the scene, making it necessary for her to clean the glass every morning.

Satisfied, she checked her watch and then switched on her curated playlist of Christmas music. If she was going to be forced to listen to holiday songs for weeks on end, it would be limited to those she could tolerate. She couldn't abide novelty songs, which was why she didn't stream one of the internet stations playing only Christmas music where she couldn't control what she heard.

She unlocked the door, flipped the closed sign to Open and waited for the first customers of the day. Sweet Briar was a tourist town that over-flowed with visitors in the summer months. Fortu-nately the mayor had great vision and had created reasons for people to visit year-round. As a result, Hannah did steady business and didn't see much drop-off during the winter months. She'd been surprised by the volume of sales her first Christ-mas and hadn't been prepared for the demand. But she'd been a fast learner. Now she stocked plenty of her exclusive clothing and jewelry for the season.

The bell over her door tinkled, signaling the arrival of a shopper.

"Come on in," she called. "Look around at your leisure."

"Oh my, look at this place. It's simply marvelous."

Hannah froze and then turned around at the sound of her mother's voice. What was she doing here? And why was she praising Hannah? Eleanor had rarely—if ever—had a complimentary word for her. Hannah and her mother had never been close. They were too different for that. Eleanor Jones-Carpenter-Halloran-Spikes had always favored Dinah, who resembled her not only in physical appearance but also in values. They were both petite, model-thin, selfish social climbers.

"What are you doing here?" Hannah noticed that her mother hadn't come alone. Dinah and Gerald were standing behind her. Dinah looked smug as usual, although Gerald had the good grace to look uncomfortable.

"I've come to see your boutique in person." Eleanor walked around the shop, admiring Hannah's designs as if the last words she'd said to Hannah—*get over it*—about Dinah and Gerald's betrayal hadn't happened. "It's beautiful. The pictures in the magazine layout last month didn't do it justice."

Hannah rubbed her head. Perhaps she'd fallen when she'd been replacing the bulb and had given herself a concussion. Or maybe she'd knocked herself out and she was lying unconscious on the floor by the jewelry display and this was an unfortunate nightmare. She glanced over there. Nope. Nothing to see there.

"Why?" If there was one thing Hannah had learned, it was that her mother had a reason for everything she did. Nothing was ever done randomly or by chance.

"Why what?"

"Why did you come all the way to Sweet Briar to see the store now?" She'd owned the boutique for nearly three years and her mother had never once been inside.

"Because you're my daughter."

"And?"

"And," Eleanor added with annoyance, "it's time for you and Dinah to put all the bad blood behind you and start acting like sisters."

Hannah didn't say a word. The idea was so ridiculous it was comical. Besides, Hannah knew her mother had an ulterior motive. She'd never cared whether Dinah and Hannah got along. All that mattered was putting on a good front. So she waited for her mother to get to the real reason they'd left Virginia in the middle of the Christmas social season when there were elbows to rub and connections to make.

"And I think the perfect gesture and symbol of this new beginning would be for you to design your sister's wedding gown."

And there it was. The real reason they'd come to Sweet Briar. Her mother and sister might enjoy playing games, but Hannah didn't have the appetite for it. She preferred honesty and straight shooting.

"No."

"What do you mean *no*?" Eleanor's perfectly shaped brows nearly disappeared into her hairline. Surely she hadn't expected a different answer.

"I mean I'm not going to design Dinah's wed-

ding dress. You've wasted your time coming here."
Hannah turned and spoke directly to her sister. "I
don't design wedding dresses, but if I did, I still
wouldn't design one for you."

"That's not true. I saw the wedding dress that
you designed for Arden Wexford. It was in all the
magazines and on every celebrity TV show. That's
all people talked about for months."

Dinah wanted her picture to be in magazines
and her face on television. It must have annoyed
her to no end to see Hannah featured as an up-
and-coming designer in a popular fashion magazine. Dinah and Eleanor hadn't cared a whit about
Hannah. But now they wanted to use their family tie, no matter how strained, in their never-
ending quest for fame and fortune. Eleanor had
used marriage as a ladder to climb to the top—or
as close to it as she could get. Now that she was
getting up there—in age as well in the number of
ex-husbands—she'd turned her attention to Dinah
as a means to that end.

"You did design that dress," her mother pointed
out.

"I also saw the gowns you made for that country singer and that movie star to wear on the red
carpet," Dinah said as if she could convince Hannah. "I'm your sister, so it's only fair that if you
design a dress for complete strangers, you should
design one for me."

Dinah seemed completely oblivious to the fact that she'd hurt and betrayed Hannah. Even for someone as self-centered as she was, this was unbelievable.

Eleanor nodded in agreement. No surprise there. Eleanor had always favored her older daughter.

Hannah folded her arms over her chest. "First, Arden isn't a stranger. She's a friend." Something Dinah and Eleanor no doubt already knew and hoped to use to their advantage. Although Hannah didn't ordinarily design wedding dresses, she'd been pleased to create Arden's.

A few years ago, Arden's car had broken down in Sweet Briar. She'd needed a break from the pressures of her prominent family, and had stayed over and worked as a waitress in her current husband's restaurant. Arden and Hannah had become friends and she'd offered to design Arden's dress. Hannah hadn't done it for fame or money, but out of friendship. It was only because Arden was a member of the wealthy Wexford family that the dress had been newsworthy. Later Arden had introduced Hannah to a couple of celebrities who'd wanted Hannah to design dresses for them. "Second, although we share the same genes, you and I aren't sisters in the true sense of the word. Sisters don't screw each other's fiancé."

Hannah knew she was being crass, but she

didn't care. She wasn't about to try to put a sweet spin on her sister's betrayal. Not when saying the words brought back the pain of that betrayal.

"Why do you have to be like that? I tried to resist. We both did, for your sake. That's why we didn't get married right away. We were considering your feelings. But Gerald and I are in love and want to be together."

Hannah managed not to throw up the yogurt she'd grabbed for breakfast. Respect for her feelings wasn't the reason Dinah and Gerald hadn't gotten married three years ago. They hadn't tied the knot because Dinah hadn't been divorced yet. Her ex-husband hadn't been in the mood to give her half of what he'd earned, so the proceedings had dragged on and on. Of course, had Dinah been as much in love with Gerald as she'd claimed, she would have just walked away from her then eight-month marriage and a huge settlement. But Dinah had absorbed their mother's teaching quite well. *Never leave a dollar behind.*

"I'm not stopping you. Get married. Have the biggest wedding the state of Virginia has seen. Heck, all of America has seen. But leave me out of it."

Gerald stepped forward then. Hannah had hoped to never see the weasel ever again. Yet here he was, standing right in front of her. He was average height with hair that was beginning to thin and cold, calculating eyes. Hannah wondered what she'd ever seen in him. When they'd worked together at his father's architectural firm, she'd been impressed by what she'd interpreted as his drive and desire to make a name for himself. Now she realized that had just been a mirage.

"Hannah, we weren't right for each other." Was he trying to sound sympathetic? If so, he was failing miserably. But then, true feelings weren't included in his limited repertoire. "I know you feel the same way."

"You got that right."

"I know you're hurt and disappointed," he said as if he hadn't heard a word she'd said. Apparently he'd prepared this speech and intended to recite every word of it. "But don't hold it against Dinah."

"You're unbelievable. Please, all of you, just leave."

"Not until you agree to make my dress," Dinah said. Clearly trying to make nice was putting a strain on her and she was reverting to type.

Hannah had a business to run. A customer could come in at any moment. She needed to put an end to this now.

"You know, I can always call the chief of police. He's a friend, too."

"You wouldn't dare," Eleanor said indignantly, pressing a manicured hand against her chest.

"Actually I would," Hannah said, hoping her

mother wouldn't call her bluff. Hannah didn't want anyone in town, especially her friends, to know about her messed up family. She'd never told a soul about them or how Gerald had betrayed her. And she never would. But Eleanor didn't know that.

"There's no need for that," Eleanor said hastily, trying to get back on script. "Hannah, just consider what's best for the family. And for you."

"How would it look if you, a successful dress designer to the stars, refuse to design a wedding dress for your only sister? It could harm your reputation if anyone ever found out how petty you're being," Dinah added.

"Was that a threat? That's an interesting strategy for someone asking a favor."

"I'm just pointing out the obvious. You like to pretend that you're the victim. Poor betrayed Hannah. The truth is Gerald dumped you because he didn't want you. He wanted me." Dinah preened as if she were some sort of prize. "You've always been jealous of my beauty. I would have thought you'd gotten over it by now. Maybe if you could find a man, you wouldn't be so bitter. But then, maybe you haven't met anyone desperate enough."

Hannah gasped. That was low even for Dinah.

The sound of a throat being loudly cleared filled the uneasy silence. Hannah closed her eyes.

Just what she'd hoped to avoid—a witness to her family's dysfunction and her personal humiliation.

She opened her eyes and turned to face her customer.

Russell Danielson. Her good friend's brother. She'd met Russell this past summer when he'd been in Sweet Briar visiting his siblings and their families. They'd hit it off and spent a glorious evening together. He'd promised to contact her when he got back to his duty station. He hadn't.

She'd been hurt when he'd ghosted her—disappointed even—but not surprised. She was still down on men. Besides, though they'd had a couple of good conversations, those talks hadn't involved anything truly personal. Still, she'd thought they'd connected. Clearly she'd been wrong.

Russell looked around the room, taking in the scene, and then smiled. Did he find the way she was standing against the wall while they circled her like sharks amusing? "Sorry I'm late."

"Uh." Late for what? Until he'd stepped into her store, she hadn't known he was in town.

He crossed the room, not stopping until he was standing an inch in front on her. Instinctively she inhaled and got a whiff of his delectable scent. He was wearing a woodsy cologne, which when mingled with his natural scent made her weak in the knees. Before she could utter a word, he put his arms around her waist and pulled her into a kiss.

His lips were warm, and the pressure was perfect. He lingered for a few seconds before pulling away. Though he'd ended the kiss, he kept his arm firmly around her waist, which was good since her knees had turned to Jell-O.

He glanced at her mother and Dinah, ignoring Gerald completely, and then back to her. "Let's take care of these customers and go somewhere to catch up."

"I can't leave. My assistant, Talia, called in sick, so I don't have anyone to cover. The mornings are busy this time of the year." How she managed to unscramble her brain well enough to formulate those sentences and force the words past her still-tingling lips was beyond her comprehension.

"Okay. I'll stick around and help."

"Who are you?" Gerald asked, as if he had a right to know.

Russell spun around slowly, drawing himself up to his full height. Though he had about six inches on Gerald, it was his demeanor that he'd perfected as a career military man that made him even more imposing. He stood erect, his powerful muscles evident under his black pressed shirt and faded jeans. He raised an eyebrow and looked Gerald up and down before grinning lazily. "Who wants to know?"

Though he spoke calmly, Russell's demeanor was no-nonsense. Gerald recognized it as well and took two steps back away from Russell before answering. "I'm Gerald Hawkins, Hannah's friend as well as her sister's fiancé."

"So we're friends now?" Hannah asked. She was sick of this circus. "I don't think so."

"I'm Dinah," Hannah's sister said, sidestepping Gerald and holding out a hand. The predatory look she shot Russell turned Hannah's stomach. Even though she and Russell weren't an item, she didn't want to stand by as her sister turned another man into a simpering fool, ready to fall at her feet. Especially since her body was still humming from that man's kiss.

Russell shook Dinah's hand and released it quickly. Dinah, who wasn't used to being dismissed so blatantly, stumbled as she stepped away. "I'm Russell Danielson. Hannah and I are dating."

They were? That was news to her. Obviously his definition of dating vastly differed from hers. But since he was standing beside her right now, looking good enough to make her sister green with envy, Hannah wouldn't complain.

"Danielson?" Her mother had been silently watching up until this point. Now her eyes glittered with avarice. Eleanor was so transparent. "Are you related to Joni Danielson who married Lex Devlin, of the cosmetic empire Devlins, and Brandon Danielson, who married Arden Wexford of the hotel Wexfords?"

"I don't generally refer to them that way," he said drily, "but yes. Joni is my sister and Brandon is my brother."

"Hannah, why didn't you tell us you were dating this nice young man?" her mother asked, all sweetness and light. "We need to get to know each other better. Perhaps we can have dinner tonight?"

"We're busy," Russell said without missing a beat.

"Then tomorrow? I won't take no for an answer. We're staying at the Sunrise B&B for the next ten days. You can leave a message for us there."

"We'll see. But don't cancel any plans you've already made."

Russell was handling this so perfectly Hannah wanted to kiss him. But then after being kissed by him once, she'd want to kiss him even if he wasn't making it plain to her family that he wasn't going to be their link to the rich and famous. His lips had been the best thing to touch hers since…well, ever. But it was time to end the shenanigans. She had a business to run and customers could walk in at any moment. Real customers who wanted to buy gifts for friends and family or for themselves.

"I hate to bring this moment to an end," she said, hoping she wouldn't get struck by lightning for telling such a boldfaced lie, "but I need to get back to work." She regretfully disentangled herself from Russell's protective arm and half shoved her family through her boutique and to the front door. "Enjoy your visit to town. And Dinah, good luck finding a wedding dress."

While Dinah gaped, Hannah flung open the door, giving them no choice but to exit. Then, although she'd just opened the shop, she switched the sign to Closed and then turned the arms on the cardboard clock indicating when she'd reopen to thirty minutes from now. Hopefully a half an hour would be enough time to regain her equilibrium.

Once her sister, mother and Gerald finally got the message that she wasn't going to unlock the door and let them back inside, they walked away, no doubt regrouping and coming up with another plan. She may not have seen Eleanor and Dinah in years, but it was evident that they hadn't changed. They were always looking to get ahead any way they could. Now that they'd met Russell, they were probably plotting a way to get their well-manicured claws into him. Gerald seemed oblivious to the fact that he might soon become disposable.

Not that Hannah felt the least bit of sympathy for him. After the way he'd betrayed her, he deserved whatever he got. Once Hannah had believed he was a good guy. He'd been charming and funny. She'd been so secure in their relationship and her belief that he'd truly loved her. Boy, had she been wrong. If she lived to be a hundred years old, she'd never forget the agony she'd felt at seeing the man who'd sworn he'd love her forever in bed with her sister.

But enough of the past and its horrible memories. She had to deal with the man currently leaning against her counter near her cash register as if he didn't have a care in the world.

Inhaling deeply and then slowly blowing out the breath, she turned. "What was that about?"

He blinked and she realized she'd snapped, taking out the frustration she felt for her mother, sister and Gerald on him. It didn't take a genius to know that he'd been trying to help her. It wasn't his fault that he'd stumbled upon an embarrassing moment for her. But she still felt humiliated, especially considering the fact that he'd gone radio silent after leaving town this past summer.

He shrugged his massive shoulders, then, unbothered, pushed to his feet. "I thought I was helping a friend. Maybe I was wrong."

"What made you think I needed your help?"

"I don't know. Maybe it was the hurt and slightly panicked expression I saw on your face when I stepped into the store. Or perhaps it was the way you were trying to back away from the barracudas encroaching on your personal space. Either answer is correct, so choose which one you prefer."

She pressed her fingers to her temples, attempting to massage away a headache that was forming.

"Just how much of the conversation did you hear?"

"Enough to know that you dodged a bullet with that guy and that your mother and sister have serious issues. Coming from that train wreck of a family, it's a miracle you're as normal as you are."

Normal. Average. Nothing special. She knew he meant it as a compliment, but it didn't feel that way. It felt like he was saying she should thank her lucky stars that she was ordinary and not as messed up as she could be. Talk about damning with faint praise.

"But you think I'm pitiful and need a fake boyfriend."

"I didn't say that."

"Not with words. But your actions sure did. As we learned in grammar school, actions speak louder than words." And though she was trying to ignore it, that kiss was definitely talking to her now. Too bad he'd kissed her out of pity.

"I thought I was helping. Your family was insulting you and I wanted to prove them wrong. Forgive me for caring."

He started to walk away and when he passed Hannah, she grabbed his arm. This conversation had gone off the rails. She was wrong to let her personal issues turn what had been a gallant gesture into something negative. "Wait a minute."

"Why?"

"I need to apologize. I understand why you pretended to be my boyfriend. To be honest, it felt good to have you stand up for me. The petty part of me was glad for them to come face-to-face with a man who was in love with me. Even if it was only pretend. But I'm not like them. I don't judge my value as a human being by my relationship status. I'm a worthwhile person whether or not I have a boyfriend."

"Of course you are. I'm sorry if my actions made you believe I thought otherwise."

"You didn't. It's just years of being treated as if I was less than Dinah by my mother has made me sensitive."

"I understand. And if you want, I'll tell them that I lied. It shouldn't be too hard to find them since we're staying at the same bed and breakfast."

"Why aren't you staying with Joni or Brandon?"

"I came to town earlier than planned and I don't want to inconvenience either of them. It'll make straightening out things with your family easy."

Hannah had the feeling there was more to it than he was letting on, but she didn't think about it for long. She was too focused on the humiliation that would follow his confession. She might not judge herself by their values, but she didn't want to be a laughingstock, either. As long as they were in town—and please let it be shorter than they'd said—she stood the chance of seeing them again. She couldn't subject herself to one more smirk. "Well, actually…"

"Actually what?"

"Now that the lie has been told, there's no reason to untell it, you know? You were trying to save me from humiliation, but setting the record straight will only lead to more."

He nodded. "Believe it or not, Hannah, I was trying to help you. I'm usually not so impulsive. In my line of work, acting without thinking can have deadly results."

"I know. Thankfully the consequences here aren't so grave." She paused for a second. "I know you probably didn't expect this to be more than a ten-minute thing. But how do you feel about continuing to be my pretend boyfriend?"

Continue to be her pretend boyfriend? Russell looked at Hannah. She appeared to be holding her breath. That beautiful face had haunted his dreams over the past five months. They'd spent only a few hours together, but he'd enjoyed every second. He'd intended to keep in touch with her when he returned to his duty station, but nothing had gone according to plan.

He'd been on a mission in the Middle East when he'd been injured in a shelling near his base. Although no one had been killed, several soldiers had sustained traumatic brain injuries. The damage to his leg, though severe, had seemed relatively minor in comparison.

Russell rubbed his knee. Though therapy had helped his injury to heal and it wouldn't hamper most civilians, he had lasting weakness from the surgery. He'd worked hard to regain his strength, but his knee had only improved so much, leaving him unable to meet the physical requirements to continue as a soldier. He'd failed his last physical and his career in the army was all but over. Once the discharge paperwork was completed, he would officially be retired from the army, his twenty-year career over. Now he was going to have to figure out what to do next.

He wasn't going to think about that now. He'd spent enough time worrying about his future. Though his friends and superiors had told him repeatedly that he needed to face facts and prepare for a new life that didn't include the army, he hadn't been ready to give up. Up until the last moment, he'd believed his leg would heal. It hadn't. Still, he didn't want to spend the next weeks brooding.

Though he hadn't planned to pretend to be Hannah's boyfriend for more than that moment—indeed he hadn't *planned* anything—it might be the distraction he needed.

He'd spent too much time worrying about his

future and the reality that the life he'd loved was ending. He'd long ago grown tired of talking about his health with his friends but there'd been no way to avoid it. Everyone on his base knew about his injury.

He'd had his fill of people commenting on his life. His friends, commanding officers, the chaplain…the list went on. Everyone had an opinion and advice. He couldn't take one more person telling him to just feel what he felt, to be in touch with his feelings.

Some, not content with that, had gone so far as to tell him what to feel. He was the first one to admit that he didn't know what he felt or where to go from here. But one thing was certain. The decision was his and his alone. If there was too much chatter, he wouldn't be able to hear his own voice. That would only lead to confusion. And he didn't want to be confused.

He'd had to get away for his peace of mind, which was why he'd come to Sweet Briar early. He hadn't told his family he was in town because he didn't want to endure listening to their advice. Or worse, their pity. Staying at the bed and breakfast temporarily would give him the privacy he craved.

"Forget I asked," Hannah said.

He'd been lost in thought so long he hadn't answered. He was the one who'd set this whole thing in motion so he should see it through to the end.

"I'd love to continue to be your pretend boyfriend. How long do you need my services?"

She looked away. "My mother said they'll be in town for ten days. I have no idea if that's the truth or just a threat."

"A threat?"

"I'm not close to my mother and sister. It might seem strange to someone who's as close to his family as you are, but I'd be perfectly happy to never see them again. I really don't think they're going to stay here for that long. They're just trying to intimidate me. Once they realize that I'm not going to break down and design a dress for Dinah, they'll leave town. At least I hope they do."

"Ten days takes us up to December 23. Two days before Christmas."

"Is that okay? I know you came to town to spend time with your family. Hopefully this won't interfere with that."

"It won't."

"I'm surprised Joni didn't mention that you were here."

"She doesn't know yet. I just got here an hour ago. You're the first person that I've seen."

"Really?" She seemed surprised. But not nearly as surprised as he was.

"Yes." He hadn't planned to stop by to see Hannah so soon. But as his rental car neared Sweet Briar, the need to see Hannah had overwhelmed him. He'd checked into the B&B and then made a beeline to the boutique.

"Do you think your family will have a problem with any of this?"

"Why would they? They like you. We'll let them believe we're dating."

"Sort of a holiday fling?"

Her voice sounded odd, but he couldn't figure out why. But then, she was good friends with his sister, Joni, and their sister-in-law, Arden. She probably hated deceiving them. But pretending to be involved with Hannah would help him, too. His family wouldn't pressure him to spend time with them when his time in town was limited. They'd believe that he and Hannah wanted to spend time alone.

"Yes."

"Are you sure you don't mind?"

"I'm positive. I started this and I intend to see it through. I'm a soldier. I've never left a mission unfinished and I don't intend to start now."

"So I'm a mission?"

"Yes. But it's top secret, okay?"

She pondered that for a moment and then held out her hand. As he shook it, something inside him that he hadn't felt in a long time stirred to life. It felt like a combination of happiness and anticipation. Both had been missing from his life for a while, so he welcomed the feeling with open arms.

Chapter Two

"So what do we do now?" Hannah asked. When she'd reopened the boutique, customers flooded the store. Russell had offered to help her until things slowed down. One hour had turned into two and in the blink of an eye the entire day had passed. She'd appreciated the help, but when she'd told him she felt guilty for keeping him from seeing his family, he'd waved away her concern like it was no big deal. She'd wondered if he was avoiding them, then dismissed the idea as ridiculous. Unlike her, he had a loving, supportive family. And for a man who'd never worked in retail and who hadn't had a clue about women's fashion, he'd done incredibly well.

A woman who'd come into the boutique looking for the perfect blouse had left with three dresses, two pairs of pants and three pairs of earrings in addition to that blouse, all because Russell had said she'd looked nice in them. He'd also given thumbs down on two other dresses and the woman had left without them.

More than providing her customers with a male's perspective, Russell had served as the muscle she'd needed, carrying boxes for her. He'd also unpacked and steamed wrinkled clothes that had arrived from the factory, something Talia would have done had she been there, and cleaned fingerprints from the window three times.

"About what?" Russell asked, leaning back in the guest chair in her tiny office. After the physical work he'd done, he should have been tired, but he looked as if he'd spent the past hours relaxing. But then he was a soldier so no doubt today had been easier than most of his days.

"About our plan. You know, pretending to date." She still felt a little bit embarrassed saying the words. It sounded desperate.

Russell had clear brown skin, beautiful dark eyes and a dimple in his left cheek. With his muscular body—broad shoulders, trim waist and strong legs—he'd probably had women chasing him most of his life. He'd never have to enter a fake relationship. She must look pitiful to him.

"I don't know. What do you usually do when you're involved with a guy? What places do you hang out here in town? Or do you generally go out of town on your dates?"

Dates? Sadly, her dates had been few and far between. It wasn't as if she was heartbroken over Gerald. She hadn't given him a thought in years. But his betrayal had hurt her badly and she wasn't ready to trust a man with her heart. She hadn't wanted to lead anyone on either, so she'd just skipped dating altogether. Life was so much more uncomplicated that way. After the chaos of her formative years, uncomplicated suited her just fine. One day there would be a place in her life for excitement and love. But not now.

"I'm up for doing anything. How about we play it by ear?"

"That sounds like a plan." Russell was silent for a moment and she wondered if he was getting cold feet. "But there is still the slight problem of how I'm staying at the same B&B as your family and whatever it is Gerald claims to be."

She couldn't fault Russell for his choice. Kristina Harrison owned the Sunrise B&B, one of two in Sweet Briar. In Hannah's estimation, the Sunrise B&B was nicer than the Come On Inn, but she could be biased. Kristina was one of Hannah's good friends and often referred her guests to the boutique. But something about Russell's arrangement puzzled her.

"I still don't understand why you're staying there. Brandon and Joni live in town. Don't you usually stay with one of them?"

A shadow suddenly crossed his face and for a moment he seemed sad. Then he blinked and his expression cleared. "I do if I'm only staying for a day or two. I'll be here for two weeks. That's too long to impose. They each have their own families. Spouses and children. The last thing they need is to have a third party getting in the way. Especially at this time of year."

"I know them, and I don't think they would mind."

He shrugged. "Probably not. But that's not the only reason I'm staying at the B&B. There's a lot going on in my life right now and I need some time on my own to think. I couldn't do that on my base, so I came here early. I love my family, but we're nothing if not opinionated. Myself included. But this is one time where I need to make a decision without everyone's input."

"It must be an important decision."

"Yes. I need to decide the next step in my future." He breathed out a long sigh. "To be honest, right now I don't know which way is up. A little peace and quiet would go a long way toward help-ing me find my way forward."

She could understand that. When she'd ended things with Gerald, her entire life had been in dis-array. That's why she'd moved to Sweet Briar to start over. Russell's situation wasn't entirely the same, but she could relate to his need for space and time on his own to come up with a plan for his future.

"Are you going to tell them you're in town??"

"Only if I have to. They aren't expecting me until next week. My parents are coming to town then too so we can celebrate Christmas together as a family. Since there's no way I can stay at the same bed and breakfast as your people with-out making them doubt that we're committed to each other, I have to find somewhere else to stay. After all, if we're involved, why wouldn't I just stay with you?"

Now she had a better understanding of his situ-ation and realized just how much having privacy at this time meant to him. Though she hadn't asked him to interfere, she was asking him to continue the charade. Right or wrong, she felt a bit respon-sible for helping him find a place to stay where he could have the time alone he wanted. "There's another B&B in Sweet Briar. Let's try and get you a room there."

"Okay."

Hannah quickly dialed the number for the Come On Inn. She requested a room and was told that there wasn't one. The answer wasn't entirely unexpected. Sweet Briar was a yearlong tourist destination. The businesswoman in her couldn't be more pleased. The woman with a dilemma found the lack of vacancies inconvenient.

She ended the call and looked at Russell.

"I take it there's no room at the inn."

"Nope. Not a nook or cranny."

He frowned and guilt pricked her conscience. He'd stepped up to help her out of a tight situation with her family. True, he hadn't anticipated the complications that could result. But still, could she live with herself if she did any less for him? She could easily help him have the time alone he needed. "I have a suggestion."

"What's that?" His eyes bored into hers.

She took a second to think. Once she said the words, there would be no taking them back. "You can stay with me."

"Stay with you?" He sounded surprised, as if the idea had never occurred to him. She hoped his astonishment didn't mean that he found the idea ridiculous. Or worse yet, repulsive.

"Yes. After all you're doing me the favor. You shouldn't have to sacrifice the time alone you need. I have a business to run and won't be at home all that much. You'll have privacy and space to think about your future."

He shook his head. "I'm the one who set this whole thing in motion by pretending to be your boyfriend. If I would have minded my own business you wouldn't be in this predicament, so I wouldn't exactly say that I'm doing you a favor."

She waved away his concern. How she'd ended up in this situation didn't matter. It was time to move forward with a credible plan. And having an adoring boyfriend stay at a B&B instead of with her made no sense and could raise her family's suspicions. "I have plenty of room. And I'd enjoy the company."

"In that case, I accept. But I think I'll hold on to my room at the B&B. It's Christmastime and I would hate for Kristina to lose that income."

"That's very thoughtful of you."

"It's only fair. So how about we go pick up my bags and bring them over to your house. Then we can grab something to eat. I'm starved."

So was she. They'd barely had time to wolf down sandwiches for lunch. And that had been hours ago.

They closed up the shop and then got into her car since he'd left his rental at the B&B and walked over the short distance earlier. When they got there, Hannah drove past the Victorian mansion and parked half a block away.

"What's wrong?"

"Did you see that silver Benz? That's my mother's. I didn't want to park near her. It would be just my luck to run into her."

"We'll have to go into stealth mode." He grinned.

"Stealth mode?" She found herself smiling back at him. When she'd first met Russell, she'd come away believing he was a strict, by-the-book military man. And in a sense he was. He took his oath and duty to serve seriously. But she'd discovered over the course of the day that he had a good sense of humor and the ability to laugh at himself, a quality she found quite appealing.

"Yes. Making ourselves invisible."

She looked down at herself. She was wearing her favorite orange blouse, a brown-and-orange patterned skirt that hit her midthigh and brown boots. There was no way she could blend into the scenery. "Look at me. I don't think that'll work."

His eyes swept over her, leaving her tingling from toes to hair. "You don't have to wear camouflage in order to be stealthy."

"Then what should I do?"

"Just act as if you belong. You'll attract more attention if you go skulking around trying to go unnoticed. But if you walk confidently through the entrance and up to my room, nobody will pay the least bit of attention to you."

"I don't know. That seems counterintuitive to me."

"Trust me, if we go hiding behind potted plants and ducking behind furniture, everyone will notice. Then they'll be on their phones telling everybody they know what they saw. Even though your mother and sister are strangers, the news will still reach them."

"You're the expert here. But you know, I could just stay in the car and wait for you."

"You could. But I have too much stuff to make one trip, which doubles the chance of me running into your mother or sister or…him."

Hannah knew that it was petty, but she thought it was hilarious the way Russell paused and didn't say Gerald's name. "You have a point. But we need to plan what we're going to say if we run into one of them. You know, in case the invisibility thing doesn't work."

He laughed. "We'll just say that we're picking up luggage for a friend. And in a way we are. That friend just happens to be me."

"But—"

"Stop overthinking," he said.

They got out of the car and then strolled down the street. They didn't see anyone, but that didn't mean they weren't seen. But since they weren't doing anything out of the ordinary, she doubted anyone paid undue attention to them. Telling herself to act as if it were perfectly normal to walk into the B&B with her pretend boyfriend, Hannah tossed her hair and stepped inside. A quick look around revealed that there were only three people in the sitting room and they were all strangers. Of course they were. Residents of Sweet Briar wouldn't need to stay at the B&B.

She and Russell made it up the stairs without incident. Hannah was confident that the mission would go off without a hitch when the door across from Russell's began to open. That wouldn't have been a problem except Hannah's sister's strident voice carried into the hallway. She was staying in that room and was on her way out.

Hannah shoved Russell's shoulder, encouraging him to pick up the pace. That had been a mistake. Her jostling made him drop the key. Visions of imminent disaster assaulted Hannah and she closed her eyes like a child playing peekaboo. If she couldn't see them, then hopefully they couldn't see her.

She felt a tug on her elbow just as her sister's voice became louder.

"You can open your eyes now."

Hannah slowly opened her eyes and looked around. She was standing in Russell's room, the door shut firmly behind her. "Did she see us?"

"No. But one second longer and she would have."

Hannah sank onto the bed. "That was close."

"Closer than it had to be." Russell sat beside her and gave her a look. "Why did you knock the key out of my hand?"

"It wasn't intentional. I heard Dinah's voice and I sort of panicked."

"Sort of panicked?"

She thought of how it must have looked from Russell's perspective and laughter bubbled up inside her. Unable to hold it back, she giggled. A moment later, she was laughing uproariously, and tears were streaming down her face.

"That was like a scene in a comedy," Russell said as he began to laugh with her. "I half expected you to start running around in circles, your palms pressed against your cheeks."

She nudged him with her shoulder. Despite her mirth, she was aware of the solid strength in his arms and the power beneath the cotton shirt. "Hey. I wasn't that bad."

He laughed again. "If only you could have seen your face. Oh wait, your eyes were closed. You couldn't see anything. I don't want to hurt your feelings, but that was the total opposite of stealth."

"So, you're saying I don't have a future as a secret agent."

"Definitely not."

She pretended to be offended. "Well, I guess everyone can't be stealthy."

"That's okay. You have plenty of other attributes." His eyes skimmed her body, sending shivers skipping down her spine. And just like that, the atmosphere went from playful to hot as sexual tension arced between them. She was suddenly aware that they were sitting on his big, comfy bed. They weren't exactly touching, but the heat from their bodies was definitely mingling. Forget sugarplums. Visions of getting closer danced in her head.

Whoa. This was just a pretend relationship. Russell was her fake boyfriend. He'd made it clear when he hadn't contacted her as he'd said he would that he wasn't interested in her. Since she wasn't open to a serious relationship either, she wasn't offended. But she wasn't going to do anything reckless, either.

Though she knew keeping their relationship strictly platonic was the right thing to do, her body rebelled, trying to tempt her into behaving foolishly. Luckily for her, Russell broke eye contact, stood and then stepped away from the bed. "I didn't unpack anything, so I just need to grab my luggage and the gifts I bought for my family."

His suitcases were leaning against an overstuffed chair. Several shopping bags filled with unwrapped presents were piled on the chair with several more stacked on the antique desk. He hadn't been exaggerating when he'd said that he'd brought more than he could carry in one trip. And given the close brush they'd had with her sister, it was best to limit his time in the B&B. Hopefully they would be able to get through the hall, down the stairs and out the door without running into any of her unwanted and unexpected visitors.

They gathered everything, then went to the door. Since there were two of them, they had an easy enough time carrying everything. Russell opened the door a crack, looked out and then glanced over his shoulder, a mischievous smile on his face. Clearly he was enjoying himself. "The coast is clear."

"So far."

"Don't be such a pessimist. We can accomplish this mission. That is if you don't knock me into a table or make a lot of noise."

"Just be sure not to attract attention." Though she hadn't mentioned it, she'd noticed the way two women in the parlor had preened when they'd looked at Russell. Since she also found him attractive, she wasn't surprised by their behavior. They'd tried to be subtle, but Hannah had noticed even if Russell hadn't. As gorgeous as he was, he was probably used to drawing women's attention.

They made it down the stairs and out the front door without seeing anyone. After the close encounter with her sister, Hannah didn't breathe a sigh of relief until they'd piled the stuff into the trunk of his car. Once they were in their separate cars, he followed her to her house, a ten-minute drive away.

When she'd moved to Sweet Briar, she'd driven around, trying to get a feel for the town. It hadn't taken her long to realize this was where she'd belonged, so she'd begun looking for a house. She'd come close to making an offer on two, but something had held her back. Neither one had felt quite right. Then one day she'd stumbled upon this house. It had been on the market for only a day, but Hannah had known the minute that she'd stepped inside that this was the home she'd been looking for.

The Victorian was filled with lots of charming nooks that added to its cozy appeal. She could feel the love the previous owners had shared with each other wrapping around her.

She unlocked the front door, picked up the bags of gifts, then stepped inside. Russell was right behind her. He looked around, his eyes moving from the sofa and chairs she'd found at an estate sale and refurnished on pleasant Saturday evenings to the antique table she'd rescued from the back of a dusty antiques shop. He let out a low whistle. "This is some place you have here."

"Thanks."

Still carrying his suitcase and stack of gifts, he stepped all the way into the front room. Although she loved every inch of her home, this room with its original hardwood floors and high windows that let in plenty of sunlight was her favorite place to spend a quiet evening or entertain friends.

"It looks like you."

"How so?"

"Warm and welcoming." His eyes held hers. "And, of course, beautiful."

Her cheeks warmed and she found herself becoming flustered. "Thank you."

They stood there for a moment in companionable silence. Then it occurred to her that Russell wouldn't ask her to show him his room. He'd simply wait politely because that's the kind of man he was. "Let me show you where you'll be sleeping."

"Thanks," he said and followed her up the stairs. The house had four bedrooms, three large ones and one small one. She'd turned the smallest one into a home office and she used another as her sewing room where she made samples of her designs to send to the factories that manufactured her clothing. The largest one was her bedroom and the room across from it was her guest room.

As they walked down the hall, she pointed out the various rooms to him so that he would feel at home. She hadn't been expecting company, so her sewing room was a bit of a mess. The dress forms that she used to size her clothes were draped with fabric for her latest designs. Remnants were strewn across the floor. Thanks to the publicity that surrounded Arden's wedding and stars who'd worn her designs on red carpets and at highly publicized events, Hannah was becoming more widely known in the fashion industry. Two national retailers were interested in carrying her clothing line. It would mean a big increase in her income, but her clothes would no longer be exclusive to her boutique. She was still weighing the pluses and minuses of the offer.

She hurriedly closed the door to her sewing room. Russell gave her a puzzled look but didn't say anything. She supposed it was an odd thing to do given that she was the one who'd initiated the tour. Still, she didn't want him looking at her mess.

"This is the room you'll be using," she said as they entered the guest room. "It's not as nice as the one at the B&B, but I hope you'll be comfortable here."

He set his suitcase on the floor by the door and she did the same. "I'll be plenty comfortable here. This room is just as nice as the room I had there. And there's no risk of running into any undesirables."

"At the B&B you would have gotten a great breakfast. The odds of that happening here are slim to none."

"I take it you don't cook."

"Not breakfast. I usually just have some yogurt or a piece of fruit. When I'm feeling fancy, I might have a bowl of cereal and a piece of toast."

"I'll be fine. But what are we going to do about dinner?"

"I made lasagna last night. There's plenty left over. I'll put together a salad and make garlic bread to go with it."

"Sounds like a plan. I can help, by the way."

"You can cook?" Hannah couldn't hide her surprise. She'd never dated a man who was willing to cook. No matter how woke they claimed to be, no matter how progressive they believed they were, they somehow took it as a given that the woman was responsible for taking care of all household chores.

"Yes. I'm not in the same category as Brandon, of course, which is why I'll never own a restaurant, but I'm never going to be at risk of starving."

They walked to the kitchen, detouring through the rooms on the first floor. The house was meant to be a family home, and with its large lot, it was a challenge for a single woman to manage, but she was happy alone here.

"This is nice," Brandon said as they stepped into the kitchen.

"Thanks." The previous owners had renovated the kitchen with granite counters and high-end appliances, so Hannah had every convenience at her disposal. Cooking here was always a pleasure.

They washed their hands and then proceeded to prepare dinner. They didn't talk much as they worked, but Hannah didn't feel uncomfortable. Quite the opposite. It was nice to be with someone who didn't feel the need to fill the silence with inane conversation.

Once the meal was ready, they sat down at the kitchen table.

"I notice you don't have a Christmas tree. Christmas is only a couple of weeks away. If you need help, I can help you get one."

Hannah frowned, wishing he'd been as content with the silence as she'd been. Because the last thing she wanted to talk about was Christmas.

Chapter Three

Russell hadn't thought his comment was all that unusual but judging by the way Hannah stiffened, he knew his offer hadn't come across as he'd intended. She seemed to withdraw into herself as if hurt. He liked Hannah and the last thing he wanted to do was hurt her. After what he'd witnessed today, he had the feeling she'd endured enough pain to last a lifetime. The way that Hannah's mother and sister had treated her was reprehensible. It was so far out of his experience that he still couldn't believe what he'd seen. That Hannah was such a sweet and generous person was nothing short of remarkable.

He'd been lucky when it came to family. His parents were loving people. They'd always supported him and his siblings in whatever they'd chosen to do. When they'd made mistakes, their parents hadn't belittled them as he'd seen the parents of some of his friends do. Instead, they'd helped them see the error of their ways and provided guidance, so they could make better decisions in the future.

He'd also been lucky in the siblings department. He, Brandon and Joni got along very well. It wouldn't be a stretch to say that they were two of his closest friends. They'd each chosen well when it came to life partners, and Russell counted their respective spouses among his friends, too. He hated to think of how hurt they would be if they knew he was avoiding them, but he couldn't take their pity over his injury right now.

"I have a tree at the store." Her voice was clipped. Cool.

"I know. I saw it. Do you intend to put your presents there?"

"What presents? I don't have kids. Or any family worth speaking of. I live alone. Though my friends and I get together and exchange gifts, I don't need to have a tree to put them under."

"That's true. But a tree is more than a place to put gifts."

"To some. But to me, it's extra work and time

I don't have to spare. It's finding a tree, shifting furniture around to make room for it, and then decorating it. I just don't have the time or the energy. To be honest, it just isn't worth the bother."

That sounded plausible. Maybe he'd misinterpreted her reaction. But judging from the expression on her face and the tone of her voice, she didn't want to discuss this subject any longer. An invisible wall had sprouted up between them, creating a barrier that he didn't want. And not simply because it would make staying in her house difficult and pretending to be her boyfriend stressful. Those were selfish reasons. The truth was, he wanted her to feel comfortable having him stay in her home. And he wanted her to enjoy the dates that he planned to take her on over the next week and a half. More than that, he wanted the smile back on her face.

He paused, his fork midway between his plate and mouth. Why was her happiness so important to him all of a sudden? He didn't know. It just was.

So he changed the subject. "What's this about you designing clothes for the stars?"

Her smile returned. "It's all a fluke."

"I doubt that."

Her smile widened and his heart began to race as if he'd run ten miles carrying thirty-five pounds of gear on his back. "It all started when Arden asked me to design her wedding dress."

"It was beautiful." Actually, he didn't remember very much about his sister-in-law's dress. He hadn't paid any attention to it. All he remembered was that it had been long and white. But he was wise enough not to say that to the person who'd designed it.

"Thank you. Anyway, she and Brandon tried to have a quiet wedding, but the press found out about it and got pictures. Of course, you were there so you already know that."

He nodded. He'd managed to get three days of leave to attend his brother's wedding. He'd missed the bachelor party, something he'd regretted, but it couldn't be helped. He'd been lucky to get the time even though two of the days had been spent traveling.

"Somehow or another the pictures of the dress ended up everywhere. Everyone wanted pictures of the rarely photographed Wexford heiress's wedding gown. They were in fashion magazines and on TV. Once Arden saw what was happening, she insisted that I be credited. Then one day out of the blue I got a call from this actress. She wanted me to design her a dress for the Academy Awards ceremony. Can you believe that? I couldn't. I thought someone was pulling my leg so I told her sure, come on down. I couldn't believe it when she actually showed up at the appointed time. Luckily I pulled myself together and designed her dress.

It was stunning if I say so myself. She wore it on the red carpet. She mentioned my name over and over. After she won the Oscar for best actress, that dress was all over the place."

"What did the critics say?"

"They all loved the dress. She was chosen as best dressed of the night. After that, I designed dresses for a couple more celebrities."

"So is this a new business for you?"

She shrugged. "I'm not about to quit my day job. It was really nice, but I don't know how many people will want me to design custom gowns for them in the future. And as much as I enjoy designing fancy clothes for those types of events, I prefer the clothes I make and sell at the boutique. Upscale clothes for the middle-class woman to wear to work and to play."

"You aren't tempted to become a designer to the stars and start hanging out with the Hollywood crowd?"

"Well, the money is nice, but I can live my life without fame and the stress that goes along with it. Can you imagine what the press would do with a family like mine? Especially since my sister and mother would like nothing better than to be famous."

"That would be a problem, but not an insurmountable one. If that's something you want to do, then go for it. Don't let them ruin your life."

"It's not what I want to do. At least not full-time. I like my life the way it is. I'm living the dream I created. I don't think I want to trade it in for a new dream. At least not now. Luckily right now I can have both."

"You are lucky. So many people don't have a clue about what they want or where they're going." Sadly, he could currently be counted among them. He didn't number himself with those who had no idea what they wanted. He did. He wanted to continue to serve his country as an active duty soldier. But what he wanted no longer mattered. He'd tried but he'd been unable to get back to where he'd been before his injury and had no choice but to retire from the army. Who would have thought that at thirty-eight he would have to start his life all over again? The life that he'd mapped out all those years ago was slipping from his grasp. People kept telling him he should be grateful that he was capable of living a normal life, but he didn't feel grateful. But since being bitter wouldn't improve his situation, he knew he would have to figure out his next move soon.

Hopefully a week alone with his thoughts would be sufficient time to devise a plan for his future. Then he would tell his family what was going on with him. If he had a plan in place, there would be no need for them to pity him.

They finished their dinner and then quickly

washed the dishes. When the kitchen was clean, they said good-night and walked upstairs to their separate rooms. Though it was early, he was sleepy and decided to call it a night. A lot had happened that day and he had a feeling there would be more drama in the days to come. He intended to be ready for it.

Hannah lay awake that night, wondering why she had behaved so impulsively that day. Ever since her childhood, which could be described as unpredictable and chaotic at best and borderline abusive at worst, she'd thought before she'd acted. She wasn't necessarily cautious, but she preferred to look at every angle and consider all possible outcomes before making a decision. Yet today, she'd behaved out of character more than once. And each time, Russell Danielson had been the catalyst.

He'd been the reason that she'd pretended they were romantically involved. Once that lie was told, she'd had to invite him to stay with her to keep up the charade. Her childhood had taught her all about the importance of her public image and she'd automatically fallen into that trap. Because of that ingrained thought process, she now had a man living in her house. Truthfully, she wouldn't have minded having Russell stay with her at any other time, like, say, the Fourth of July. She liked him and enjoyed his company. But Christmas was different from any other holiday. Whereas other holidays lasted a day, Christmas had an entire season and numerous traditions.

Once, she'd loved Christmas and everything about it. She'd loved the music and the lights and baking dozens of Christmas cookies shaped like elves and stars. She'd arranged her schedule so that she could watch her favorite holiday specials whenever they'd been on TV. Hannah had been the one to organize her friends to go caroling at senior citizen centers and hospitals. She'd been the one to arrange Secret Santa exchanges and tree-trimming parties with her friends. But that was then. Now she couldn't wait for the season to be over.

When her plan to get married on December 22, combining her wedding and her favorite holiday, had gone up in flames, the entire season had lost its appeal. As a business owner, she couldn't ignore the season in her shop. People expected and enjoyed the decorations and the music. So she'd sucked it up and decorated her store. She played Christmas music from the moment the boutique opened until she closed for the night. Since she didn't want to explain her lost love for the season to her neighbors and friends, she'd decorated the outside of her house with the minimum amount of lights that she could get by with without leading to questions. But inside? Not one chrysanthemum, or light, or tree. This was her sanctuary.

Despite lacking the outward signs of Christmas, she was still reminded of the wedding that wasn't. The absence of Christmas decorations hadn't made the season vanish. Nor had it diminished her pain. But since she couldn't think of another way to deal with her hurt, she would continue on this way.

Even though Russell had let the matter drop at dinner, she knew he'd have more questions. She would in his position. But whether or not he would ask them remained to be seen. Russell was a gentleman, but he was also direct, a quality she admired. She knew he wouldn't tiptoe around her or beat around the bush. She could make up something, or she could tell him the truth. After all, he'd already had the pleasure of making the acquaintance of her family. After that, nothing she said could shock him. Surely he would understand how she felt.

Or would he? People could be quick to minimize others' pain. It wasn't all that unusual. In fact, she'd been guilty of it herself. Once or twice things that had been heartbreaking and devastating to her friends hadn't seemed like a big deal to her. Fortunately she'd been able to pick up the hurt in her friends' voices and on their faces in time to make a course correction, saving her from saying the wrong thing.

Though she didn't want to put too much emphasis on Russell's reaction, she knew it would make a difference in their friendship. She wanted him to understand—not judge. They might only be pretending to have a relationship, but still, it was important that he respect her feelings. She would never accept less than that from a real boyfriend and she wouldn't accept it from a pretend boyfriend, either.

But she'd thought about it enough for one night. Tomorrow would be busy, so she needed to get some sleep.

The smell of bacon reached Hannah's nose and she sat up, turning off the alarm before it was set to go off. She shook her head, chasing away the cobwebs. For a minute she wondered if she was imagining the smell. She inhaled again. No. That was the unmistakable aroma of bacon.

She grabbed her robe from the hook inside her closet, wrapped it around her shoulders and shoved her arms into the sleeves as she crossed the room. As she descended the stairs and headed toward the kitchen, other smells joined the heavenly scent of bacon. When she reached the doorway, she leaned against the wall and watched as Russell pulled a pan of biscuits from the oven and set it on the counter. He spun around and caught a glimpse of her staring at him.

He smiled. "Hey."

"Good morning."

"I thought I'd make you a good breakfast before you went off to work. After spending the day working with you, I know how much effort it takes to keep that boutique going."

His thoughtfulness warmed her and set her heart aflutter. "Thank you so much for cooking. Give me a couple of minutes to wash up and I'll be right back."

"Okay. Food will be on the table in five."

Nodding, she turned and dashed from the room and up the stairs to the bathroom. She washed her face, brushed her teeth and ran a comb through her hair before returning to the kitchen. There wasn't enough time to change out of her pajamas, so she pulled the belt on her robe tighter and went back to the kitchen.

Russell was just putting the plates on the table as she stepped into the room.

"Just in time," he said, then pulled out a chair for her.

"Thank you," she said as she sat down. The small courtesy touched her heart more than she would have expected. It wasn't as if he'd presented her with a bouquet of red roses and a box of chocolate-covered strawberries.

Russell sat across from her. Dressed in a long-sleeved gray pullover that stretched over his muscular shoulders and loose-fitting faded jeans that emphasized his strong thighs, he made her mouth water more than the food on her plate. They might be just friends, but she wasn't blind.

And that face? Whew. With smooth brown skin, big dark brown eyes rimmed with long soot-black lashes and that dimple, his features were strong and attractive. Manly. She realized where her mind was wandering and quickly made a U-turn. She wasn't going to make the mistake of falling for her pretend boyfriend. Doing so could lead to real pain, something she'd had quite enough of. Scooping up a forkful of fluffy scrambled eggs, she gave them a taste.

"These are delicious."

"Don't sound so surprised. I come from a long line of great cooks." He bit into a buttery biscuit. After chewing it, he continued. "Well, maybe the line isn't all that long. My grandfather owned a soul food restaurant on the south side of Chicago. I didn't hang out there as much as Brandon, who loved to cook—obviously, since he's a chef and owns a restaurant—but I still learned a thing or two from my grandfather."

"Your parents still live in Chicago, right?"

"Yes. They love it there. Though they come here

to visit Brandon and Joni and their families, there's no way they'll leave Chicago. That's their home."

"What about you? Where is your home?"

He frowned as if his flaky biscuit had suddenly turned into cement. As he'd done last night with his question about her lack of a Christmas tree, she'd touched a nerve though she couldn't fathom how. The little bit of time they'd spent together this past summer clearly hadn't been enough time to get to know each other. But then, couples in real relationships had to discuss tough topics. Since theirs wasn't a real relationship, she probably should just let the subject drop.

Or should she? Theirs might not be a real romance, but she would like for them to be friends and not merely acquaintances. While she was deciding what to do, he answered.

"I don't really have a hometown right now. I've been in the military most of my life and traveled wherever I was needed. I've gone from base to base, country to country. Right now, I'm stationed in Germany. When I had leave, I generally returned to Chicago. Of course, Joni and Brandon were still living there as well as my parents, so it was a no-brainer. But Joni and Brandon have families and they've settled in Sweet Briar so Chicago is a bit different now."

"I imagine it would be." Though he'd spoken without the least bit of self-pity, it sounded a bit lonely, a feeling she was all too familiar with. Of course, hers was a different kind of loneliness. She'd made a hometown here in Sweet Briar but lacked a family. Friends were wonderful and she loved hers, but they could never replace blood relatives. But she was better off without her mother and sister in her life.

When she'd been a kid, she would wish on stars for a better family. With each successive stepfather, she'd hoped for a change in her situation. Her own father had died when she was only three years old, but she remembered feeling loved and cherished by him, a feeling she'd never quite had with her mother. But then, her mother had had Dinah to love. Even then Dinah had been a clone of their mother in both looks and attitude. Hannah had been different. She'd never shared or even understood their values.

"Do you like a certain kind of place? Are you a big-city person or do you prefer small towns? Can you picture yourself living on a ranch? Farming? Or maybe living on a houseboat? Pulling a camper so you can see the country?"

He chuckled at that last bit as she'd intended. There was a heaviness in the air. She didn't want it to cast a pall over the day. He'd started the morning by preparing this thoughtful breakfast, and she wanted the joy that had sprouted in her heart to touch his heart, too.

"Well, I can safely say that traveling across the country isn't something that I want to do in the immediate future. Maybe I'll reconsider in thirty or so years. Same as the houseboat. Not that there's anything wrong with people who choose to live that way."

"Of course not."

"But I've spent a good deal of my life moving around so the idea of putting down roots has appeal. Now where exactly? That's a different question. I know I would like to be near my family."

Of course he would. That was one of the things that she admired about Russell. He loved his family and enjoyed their company. "That narrows it down to two places. But the funny thing is, the two places are wildly different. Chicago is a big city with millions of people. I've never been there myself, but I know there are lots of things to do there. Sweet Briar is a small town of a few thousand citizens. It moves at an entirely different pace. There's an energy here because there is energy everywhere, but it's not the same as Chicago.

"And you wouldn't have to live in town. There are ranches nearby if that's your thing."

"I've spent a lot of time in tight quarters, so I like the idea of having room to move around. Now, do I need acres and acres of it?" He shook his head. "No. Besides, what I know about raising cattle or horses can fit on the back of a bottle cap, as my grandfather used to say. And I have no interest in learning."

"So I won't be seeing you in a cowboy hat?"

"I didn't say that. I might be able to rock a Stetson. Maybe grow my beard out some."

She suddenly imagined him as he described himself, and she had to admit he looked pretty good.

"A ranch would be too big, a camper or houseboat too small." He looked around her kitchen. "I think your house is just right."

"Hold your horses, Goldilocks. This house is perfect—for me. And it's not for sale."

He pushed his empty plate into the center of the table and then leaned against the back of his chair. He gave her a wicked grin that made her toes curl. "Well, I guess I'll just have to persuade you to let me stay here a bit longer."

Her heart skipped a beat. The idea held appeal. What would it be like to come home from work every day knowing that Russell would be there and they'd spend the evening together? She forced the idea from her mind before it could take root. He'd been kidding. He was here because she hadn't kicked her toxic family to the curb as she should have. If she'd more definitively cut ties years ago, she wouldn't be in this predicament. After all, she's the one who'd told her mother where she was moving. It had been a ridiculous moment of weakness.

She'd actually told herself that her mother would care and want to keep in touch. She hadn't contacted Hannah once. At least until she'd wanted something for Dinah, the daughter she loved.

"Hey, I was joking," Russell said, and she realized she hadn't replied.

"Were you? Because I was calculating your share of the mortgage. Of course, if I wake up to breakfast this good every day, I might not charge you a cent. In fact, I might just lock you in the house and hold you hostage."

He crossed his muscular arms over his equally muscular chest. "Is that right? And how do you propose to do that?"

"I'll overpower you. I may be smaller than you, but I'm mighty."

"Lucky for us, we don't have to see if you'll be able to pull that off. I'm more than willing to do the cooking while I'm here. And if you play your cards right, I might put a couple of things in the freezer when I leave."

"Assuming I let you leave."

They laughed together and rose.

"I'll take care of the dishes," he said as he took her empty plate and coffee cup from her hands. "I imagine you need to get going if you're going to get to work on time."

She looked at the clock on the stove. Where

had the time gone? If she didn't hustle she'd be late. "Thanks."

As she raced from the room, one thought stayed with her. She could easily get used to having Russell around.

And that was a problem. She didn't want to get used to having him around when she knew he would be leaving.

Chapter Four

Russell made quick work of cleaning the kitchen and was at the front door in time to say goodbye to Hannah before she left for the boutique. He'd brewed a fresh pot of coffee and had filled a travel mug he'd found in a kitchen cabinet.

"Thanks." She sounded surprised as she took the mug from him with one hand and held out the other. "Here's an extra set of house keys in case you want to go out."

"Thanks. I appreciate it."

"See you tonight."

"See you later." He watched her get into her car and drive away before closing the door.

Hannah might not have paid attention to what he'd said, but it didn't matter. He was going to see her before tonight. In fact, he intended to see her in a few hours. But there were still things he needed to do before he showed up at the boutique to help her and then buy her lunch. If yesterday was a typical day, he had a feeling she wouldn't eat unless he provided her with the food. Hopefully they'd scared off her horrid family and they'd left town. Of course, the odds of that happening weren't that great. He'd encountered more than his share of selfish jerks and they'd rarely given up after being shot down the first time. More than likely her family had put their heads together and were trying to come up with a better strategy for advancing their agenda. Too bad for them he was an excellent strategist and would foil each of their plots. Nobody was hurting Hannah on his watch.

Although their friendship was new, he cared about Hannah. And it was easier to concentrate on solving her problem than it was to focus on his. There were actions he could take to help her. They had a plan and a strategy to execute it. When they'd checked every item off the to-do list, they would have achieved their goal.

He was far from coming up with a strategy to solve his problem. There were just too many unknowns. His entire life was in shambles and he had no idea which item to conquer first. As someone who was used to having a mission and a plan, his whole life suddenly felt foreign and he was fighting to keep it from descending into chaos. No matter how strong his will and dedication, no matter how hard he tried, he hadn't been able to strategize his way to good health so he could live the future he'd planned.

It wasn't in his nature to stand around brooding, hoping the answers would magically occur to him. He had a mission to accomplish. He wouldn't convince Hannah's family that he was her devoted boyfriend by standing around here. There was a romance to plan.

At thirty-eight, he'd never met a woman who'd made him want to give up his career. Such a woman probably didn't exist. Now that his career was coming to an end, he wondered if he'd missed something. Had he overlooked the woman who would have made his life complete? Had he discarded a relationship he should have held on to? There was no sense in looking back since he couldn't change anything. He had to start where he was. Once this fake relationship was over, there would be plenty of time to find a woman to spend the rest of his life with.

It was a nice day, so Russell changed into black shorts and a gray army T-shirt to jog around the neighborhood. At this time of day he knew Brandon would be at the fish or produce markets and

Joni would be at the youth center where she was the director, so the chance of running into either of them was slim to none. Although Sweet Briar was a small town, it covered a lot of area and was spread out. For the most part the houses were on good-sized lots.

He hadn't been kidding when he'd told Hannah that her house was just the right size for him. Though he hadn't decided whether to settle in Sweet Briar with his siblings or return to Chicago where his parents still lived, he knew he wanted a house with plenty of bedrooms on a good-sized lot. His time of living in a Cracker Jack box was in the past.

As he jogged, he passed a woman pushing a giggling toddler in a stroller and smiled. For the first time in his life he wondered what it would be like to have a child. Not the responsibility part. He knew all too well what it was like to be responsible for someone else and the stress that came with knowing that one false move could result in irreparable harm—or death—to that person. No, he was more curious about how it felt to have your own child put their chubby arms around your neck and hug you. Or to have that child scribble a picture just for you. He'd gotten lots of gifts from his nephew and niece and he treasured them. He enjoyed being Uncle Russell. But at thirty-eight, he was starting to believe that he might like to be *Daddy*, as well.

He pushed himself to run a little faster, turning the idea over in his mind. Though it was a new one that had apparently come out of nowhere, it seemed to fit. Of course, if he was going to make the notion into reality, it was going to take some action on his part. But would a woman be interested in a man who was going to be forced to start over from scratch?

Although he'd joined the military straight out of high school, he'd gotten college degrees in counseling and child psychology while serving. He'd never intended to use the degrees. He'd just been interested in the subject. Since he was about to join the civilian workforce, he might have to put the degrees to use.

In that case, moving to Chicago would make a lot more sense than staying here in Sweet Briar. There would be more job opportunities there than here. But if he lived in Chicago, he wouldn't be able to see Hannah on a regular basis. That thought brought him up short and he slowed his pace. Was he really planning his future around his ability to spend time with his fake girlfriend? He'd lived his life without her. Until they'd met this past summer, he hadn't known she'd existed. How had she become so important to him all of a sudden? He'd give that some thought later. Right now he had to get back home.

When he returned to Hannah's house, he took a quick shower. He'd just gotten dressed when his cell phone rang. The thought to just ignore it briefly crossed his mind, but he couldn't. It might be an emergency. Or Hannah could be calling. Perhaps her mother or sister had stopped by the boutique and was harassing her. Or maybe after seeing Hannah again, her ex had realized he'd chosen the wrong sister and wanted a second chance. Not that he believed for a minute that Hannah would take the jerk back. She was much too smart for that.

But maybe she still loved him. That would explain why she was so heartbroken after all this time. Love could make a fool of even the wisest woman. The thought of Hannah and Gerald made Russell's blood boil and his hand curled into a fist. Why was he reacting like this? The whole notion was a figment of his imagination.

The phone rang again, pulling him back into reality. He barked *hello* into the phone.

"Did I catch you at a bad time?"

Russell recognized the army chaplain's voice and frowned. Over the course of the past two years, he and Major Anthony had become friends. They'd often worked out together and frequently got together to shoot pool. Major Anthony was the only person who'd had a winning record against him. If Russell hadn't known better, he'd think the chaplain had hustled pool in a former life. Though they hadn't spoken in a while, Russell had a feeling his old friend wasn't calling to catch up.

He blew out a breath. He didn't want to have this conversation. But knowing his friend, he wasn't going to get out of it. Either they talked now, or they would talk later. Knowing that Major Anthony meant well was one of the things that kept him from ending the call. Respect was the other. "No. I can talk."

"Good. So how is your family?"

"I haven't seen them yet."

"No? Why not? You made it home safely, didn't you?"

"You know I did." Russell went into the living room and sat down on a slip-covered chair near the unlit fireplace. He didn't know why but being in Hannah's space relaxed him. It was as though she was there, wrapping her arm around his waist, leaning her head against his chest and assuring him that everything would be all right. Since he anticipated the conversation being an uncomfortable one, he may as well be physically comfortable.

"Then why haven't you seen your family yet?"

"That's a long story."

"Lucky for you I have time."

Russell sighed. "I bet you do. The reason I haven't seen my family is that I'm trying to figure out my future. I'd prefer to do that without their input."

"But it's Christmas. They'll want to see you."

"And they will. They aren't expecting me for a few days."

"So where are you? Please tell me you aren't holed up in some hotel somewhere."

"No. I'm in Sweet Briar. I'm actually staying with a friend." Russell tried to sound normal but even he heard the way his voice softened on the word *friend*. Apparently even talking about Hannah affected him.

"I take it that this friend is a woman."

"It's not like that between us. She's just a friend." A friend who he was pretending to be involved with. A friend whose kiss had sent enough bolts of electricity surging through his body to light every tree in this town. Closing his eyes, he recalled just how soft her lips had been. How warm. When he'd wrapped her in his arms, he hadn't been thinking about protecting her from the hurt her family was inflicting. That had initially been his goal, but with just one touch, his mind had changed. He'd *wanted* to kiss her. *Needed* to kiss her. Truth be told, he wanted to kiss her again and was going to create as many opportunities to do just that.

That thought brought him up short and he immediately shot it down. Kissing Hannah would only lead to complications he didn't need right now.

"So when did you meet her? And why haven't I heard about her before now?"

"Her name is Hannah and I met her when I visited my family this past summer." Back before the pieces of his world had blown apart. Back when his life had held promise. He'd experienced happiness with her that he hadn't found with anyone else before. At the time, he hadn't been looking for it. Now he longed to find that peace and contentment again, which was why he'd sought her out as soon as he'd gotten to town. Kissing her had been an unexpected bonus.

"Ah. So you went back to see her instead of seeing your family. What does she have to say about everything?"

"I haven't told her anything yet."

"You can't build a relationship on a foundation of secrets."

"I'm not building a relationship with her." At least not in the sense the major meant. Their relationship was strictly pretend. And that was the way it had to remain.

"No? But you're staying with her. Does she run a rooming house or something?"

"No. I just needed some space and she's giv-

ing it to me. That's all there is. No more. No less."
What he'd just said might not be the absolute truth,
but it wasn't a lie, either. Yes, she was giving him
space and there wasn't more to it now. But there
was the possibility that something might happen
between them in the future. If Russell ever got
his life straightened out. That thought surprised
him. He couldn't believe he was thinking about
her this way so soon.

"Okay. I'm glad to hear that you're taking time
to think about your future. You still have a great
one, by the way."

"Just not the one that I planned."

"Maybe not, but there's no saying it can't be
good. You just have to decide to make the best of
it. Find the positive."

"And if there isn't one?"

"There is. If you know where to look. Being a
soldier required you to make a lot of sacrifices.
There were things you couldn't do. Now you're
going to have a different life than the one you'd
planned, and new opportunities. That is if you
open yourself up to the possibility. Whatever you
do, don't become bitter."

Russell wasn't worried about that. He'd joined
the military with his eyes open and knew the life
he'd lived could end—or change—at any time.
True, the reason he'd joined no longer existed, but
he'd discovered early on that he'd liked being in

the army. He liked the structure. The discipline. The challenge of becoming better every day. He liked having a defined mission to accomplish and a method of getting it done. Now, through no fault of his own, that life was over. He wasn't bitter. Just disappointed that the end had come so soon and without warning. Now he had to find another path in life. Another mission to fulfill. That is, after he accomplished his current mission with Hannah.

"You don't have to worry about that. I know all good things end."

They talked for a few more minutes, but happily didn't talk further about Russell's future. There wasn't anything new to say and he didn't feel like rehashing old conversations. New ideas or solutions weren't going to magically materialize and solve his problem. Only thinking and planning would do that, something he wasn't inclined to do now.

Russell promised to keep in touch and ended the conversation, then pulled himself together. It was time to be Hannah's boyfriend.

Truth be told, he didn't have that much relationship experience for a man his age. His first love, his high school sweetheart, had broken his heart. When Tricia had told him she was pregnant, he'd known it was time to grow up. He'd joined the army so he would be able to support her and their child. Two weeks later she'd miscarried. They'd stayed together for a few more weeks, but with nothing to tie them together except their shared grief, she'd broken up with him.

The following fall he'd left for basic training and she'd gone away to college. He hadn't heard Tricia's name in nearly twenty years and hadn't thought of her in nearly as long. Still, he hoped she'd lived a good life and was happy.

It had taken his broken heart a while to mend, but eventually it had. He'd soon learned that life in the military wasn't conducive to successful relationships. At least not for him. The army had been his mistress. He'd traveled a lot, going from one base to another every two or three years. The unpredictability of his lifestyle made maintaining a romance difficult. And truth be told, he'd never met a woman who'd made it worth the effort. As a result, his life had been filled with temporary, no-strings-attached relationships. Neither party had expectations of building a future together. These were the stick-around-as-long-as-the-fun-lasts type of relationships.

Now Russell wished he'd found someone with whom he could share more than a good time. He wanted a partner. Someone by his side in good times and bad. Someone to count on when the going got tough. Once he got his life back on track and had something to offer, he'd make it his mission to find a woman like that. But first he had to sort out his life. It wouldn't be fair to bring a woman into this confused and unsettled mess.

Deciding that he'd had enough introspection for one day, he headed to the boutique to help Hannah. He smiled at the thought of seeing her again. She really was a sweet woman and definitely worth getting to know better.

"Are you sure this doesn't come in purple? The color looks great on me. Everyone says so."

"I'm positive," Hannah said, managing to hold her smile in place. Every once in a while she encountered a difficult customer. This woman could be counted among the worst.

Hannah didn't believe clothes should be restricted by age or size. In her opinion, people should wear clothes that made them feel good. By the same token, she reserved the right to design clothes in the colors and patterns that she preferred. The cocktail dress the woman was holding came only in black, silver or gold.

The woman frowned. Clearly she wasn't used to being told no.

"Maybe you should get it in gold, Yvette," her long-suffering husband said. When the couple had entered the boutique, he'd taken a seat in one of the chairs Hannah had grouped in front of the window. Quite frequently her shoppers were accompanied by spouses or significant others who preferred to read one of the newspapers or magazines she'd placed on the table or to people-watch through the window. He'd been a people-watcher. Until Yvette had insisted that he trail her around the shop, carrying the clothes that she wanted to try on.

"I don't want it in gold. I want it in purple." She stomped her foot like a spoiled child, then turned back to Hannah. "I'd like to speak to your manager."

"What?"

"Your manager. I'd like to speak to her. Now."

"That would be me. In fact, I'll do you one better. I'll let you speak to the owner. Also me."

Yvette's jaw dropped. "You? But you're so young."

Hannah smiled. She was used to that, so she wasn't offended. She raised her right hand. "Scout's honor."

"So you're telling me this doesn't come in purple."

Did the woman actually think that by saying the same thing over and over she'd get a different answer? "No. Only the colors that you see."

"Well, maybe I'll just try someplace else. Perhaps a larger store will have the dress in purple."

"I can guarantee you that they won't."

"Why is that?"

"Because I designed the dress. This is the only place where you'll be able to buy my clothes."

The woman looked perturbed for a moment. For a second Hannah thought she would put back the three other dresses she'd tried on and sworn she couldn't live without. Then her eyes gleamed. "Are you saying that there's no other place in the country that carries any of these clothes?"

"The ones labeled Designs by Hannah."

The woman walked to the wall where Hannah had hung up framed photos of the celebrities wearing the dresses she'd created for the red carpet events. "Did you design these?"

"I did."

The woman smiled, took the dresses from her husband and pointed to the chair he'd reluctantly vacated. "Sit down, Henry. I've got a lot more shopping to do. Those stuck-up women at the country club are going to be green with envy when I show up in Designs by Hannah."

Hannah smiled as the man practically danced back to his chair. "I'll hold those dresses if you're sure you want them."

"Oh I absolutely want them. I think I'll get one of everything in the store that's in my size. Those old biddies will rue the day they looked down their noses at me. New money, indeed."

Hannah imagined what the woman meant by that comment and she felt a bit of sympathy for her. Nobody liked to be rejected.

Three more customers entered, and Hannah

once more wished Talia had been well enough to work today. The Christmas rush was more hectic this year than it had ever been. In addition to the ads she regularly placed in the *Sweet Briar Herald*, she'd taken out ads in newspapers in the three surrounding states. It was her way of supporting local newspapers that were struggling to compete with online news and national papers. Judging by the number of out-of-town shoppers she'd had, that investment was paying off. Of course, many of the customers had seen her gowns on TV and in the fashion magazines. While she hadn't created a knock-off dress for any of the designs, her new line of formal dresses had been flying off the racks.

Hannah helped the customers find gifts for friends all the while keeping an eye on Yvette's growing pile. She hadn't been kidding when she'd said she was going to buy one of every item that fit. Once she tried on the last blouse, she and Henry approached the counter. Hannah had to give the man credit. He didn't even blink when Hannah handed him the bill. He simply slid his debit card into the reader, punched in his security code and then returned the card to his wallet.

Hannah hung the clothes on hangers and then placed them in personalized garment bags. Smiling, she handed over the items. "Enjoy the rest of your day."

Yvette grinned. "Honey, wearing these clothes, I'm going to enjoy a lot of days."

After they left, Hannah leaned against the counter. Between Yvette and the other customers who'd come into the boutique that morning, the store was looking pretty disheveled. Hannah felt the same. She'd tried to return items to their proper racks whenever she'd had a chance, but it was difficult to keep the store organized with people constantly picking up garments and setting them wherever they happened to be standing at the moment.

Since the store was currently empty, she went to the changing rooms and gathered clothes that had been left there. Some had been neatly placed on hangers, but several blouses and a skirt had simply been dropped onto a bench. Sighing, Hannah picked them up. They were wrinkled and needed to be steamed before she could return them to the racks.

The bell over the door tinkled and she rushed to the front to greet her new customers. When she saw Russell standing there, she smiled. "Hi. What are you doing here?"

"I'm here to help. I remember how busy you were yesterday and figured you could use another pair of hands. And when you get hungry, I'll run out and pick up lunch."

At his mention of yesterday's visit, she recalled

the kiss and her heart skipped a beat. It would almost be worth having her annoying family barge in again if their presence meant she'd get to kiss him again.

"That would be great. If you don't mind carrying in a few boxes. I had a busy morning and sold a lot more than I expected to. Since I have a quiet moment now, I can do some restocking."

"Sure. I can do that. Just show me where everything is."

Hannah led him to the storage room at the back of the building. When she'd first opened the boutique, she'd decided that the smallest room would be good for storage. At the time, she hadn't anticipated her business growing as rapidly as it had so she hadn't thought she'd need much space. She opened the door and led him inside. Boxes were piled high, nearly reaching the ceiling. The room, which was small to begin with, suddenly felt no bigger than a shoebox. Russell was standing so close to her that she inhaled his enticing scent with every breath.

He stared at her and she wondered if his mind was replaying the kiss as hers was doing. His lips lifted into a smile that was sexier than it had a right to be. "What do you need me to move?"

She blinked and chased away the ridiculous notion of making out in the storeroom. For heaven's sake. She wasn't a sixteen-year-old girl sneaking off to make out with her boyfriend. She was a grown woman with a business to run. Turning, she walked down the aisle between the stacks of boxes, reading the labels and pointing to the ones she needed. He nodded and grabbed a pen from the tiny desk by the door and marked the boxes as they went. When they reached the back wall, she spun around. He was standing mere inches away from her. If she reached out, she could touch him.

"Would you please bring them into the work room? That way I can steam out the wrinkles and hang them up."

"Sure. I can help you get out the wrinkles if you need me to."

She did have two steamers, so working together, the job would be finished twice as fast. But the workroom was small, and she didn't know how long she could be in tight quarters with him before giving in to temptation. Theirs was a fake relationship. But she realized she needed to clarify the terms of their fake relationship. Did they pretend to be involved only when her family was around? Or did they keep up the pretense whenever they had an audience? Suddenly she wished they'd established parameters before now. She didn't like feeling off-balance. She needed clarity. There was no time like the present to set everything straight.

Before she could utter a word, the bell over her front door chimed, followed by female voices.

"I need to get out front. If you'll get the garments out of the box and place them on hangers, that would be a big help. We can take care of steaming them later."

"Okay."

She took a step and stopped. When he realized he was keeping her from passing, he moved aside. The space was narrow and though she tried to keep from touching him, she didn't want to make it obvious. She brushed against his arms and electricity shot through her body, making her shiver. She murmured a quick *sorry* before sprinting from the room, not stopping until she was in the front of the shop.

What an idiot. She must have looked like a crazy person running away like that. Or worse, the stereotypical maiden aunt, appalled by merely touching a man. She shook her head, trying to shake the picture from her mind. She didn't even want to imagine what Russell was thinking of her right now. No doubt he was trying hard not to laugh too loudly.

Thankfully there were customers who needed her assistance, giving her something to focus on so she wouldn't brood about how pathetic she'd appeared.

"I love this blouse," a woman with a sleek bob said. "Do you have it in medium?"

"I do. I'll need to get it from the back. If there's anything else you'd like to try on, feel free to do so. I'll only be a minute."

The woman nodded and headed over to the racks while Hannah returned to the back of the store. When she got there, Russell was leaning against the wall, using it for support as he rubbed his right knee.

"Are you okay?"

Grimacing, he jerked to a standing position. "I'm fine. I just twisted my knee."

"Are you sure that's all?" she asked, hurrying to his side. She automatically touched his knee, trying to see exactly how he'd hurt himself. "It looks a little bit more serious than that from my point of view."

He brushed her hand aside. "I told you I'm fine. If you're worried that I'm going to sue you, don't be."

"The thought never crossed my mind." She rose to her full height. In her heels, she was only a few inches shorter than he was, so they were nearly eye to eye. Much better than being bent over his knee. "And why are you acting like a jerk?"

"I'm not. You're making too big a deal of this. You're not really my girlfriend, so stop acting like it. There's nobody around to see."

She reeled back. His words were a slap in the face. Perhaps he'd noticed the way she'd reacted to being near him and wanted to make sure she knew the score. "Message received. Loud and clear. But let me point out that you're the one who started this entire farce. I had control of the situation with my family before you came charging in here like some overly zealous knight in shining armor."

He blew out a breath, then shook his head. "I'm sorry. That was totally uncalled for. You don't deserve to be treated like this."

"You're right. I don't."

"Please forgive me."

She hesitated. Their friendship was new, but she did value it. And she wanted to get to know him better. It was clear that he was in pain, which could explain in part why he'd lashed out. But still, she didn't intend to become his punching bag. "This time I will. But don't make a habit of taking out your bad mood on me."

"I won't."

She turned to leave but he stopped her. "You came in here for something and I know it wasn't just to check up on me."

"Right. I need a blouse for a customer." Although Russell hadn't emptied all of the boxes, he'd removed the blouse she'd needed. Not only that, he'd steamed it along with several others and placed them on satin padded hangers. She grabbed the blouse she needed. "This is what I came for. Thanks."

"No worries, boss."

She walked from the room. There was something going on with Russell that made her worry. But she didn't have time to figure it out now. Maybe later. And if he got upset at his pretend girlfriend for crossing the line? She'd deal with it. What was the worst that could happen? He couldn't break her heart.

At least she hoped not.

Chapter Five

"Whew. Made it through another day." Hannah closed and locked the door behind the last customer and then leaned against it. She was so exhausted she could sink to the floor and go to sleep then and there.

"Did you think you wouldn't?" Russell asked. She knew he had to be tired, but he stood erect. No doubt his military training had something to do with that. Inanely she wondered if that training had anything to do with how his clothes were still pressed and neat. If she didn't know better, she'd think he'd snuck off and ironed them sometime during the day. But she did know better. There hadn't been time.

"When that tour group walked in, I had my doubts. Who knew that having my dresses in fashion magazines would translate to such an increase in business? Honestly, I don't think most of the people who came in here even knew what kind of clothes I design. I think they were hoping to get a glimpse of a celebrity."

"Maybe that's why they came in originally. But did you see the way they swarmed the racks? Clearly they weren't only interested in buying something from a designer to the stars. They tried on lots of clothes and bought most of them."

"That's true. And they did decide not to buy clothes that didn't work for them. Especially after you made a comment or two."

"I hope that was okay to do. The last thing I want to do is cost you sales."

"You were right. The first dress the redheaded woman tried on didn't showcase her assets the way the second dress did. Besides, she did ask." Hannah pushed away from the door and went back to work. There was still a lot to be done before she could call it quits for the night. "If you ever decide to give up this army gig, you have a future in retail."

He frowned briefly before his smile returned. "I just know what looks good on a woman."

She liked to think that she did, too. Though her customers often asked for her opinion, once Russell had shown himself willing to give a man's perspective, it was as if she'd become invisible. The women had lined up to hear what he had to say. Thankfully he really did have a good eye.

"So two days in a boutique and you're an expert?" Hannah teased.

"Two days plus thirty-eight years of being male." His eyes roved over her body from shoes to hair, taking their own sweet time. By the time he was finished, her face was hot and her skin was tingling. "Now take you, for example."

"Let's not." Hannah had spent her formative years having her appearance judged and found lacking by her mother. Whereas her mother and sister were delicate and petite, Hannah was five foot seven and curvy. It was only after she'd reached adulthood that she'd realized that her mother's opinion was warped. It had taken her a while to gain a healthy self-image, which was why she was careful not to harm others with hurtful comments. And it was why her clothes came in all sizes and styles to make all body types look good.

"You dress sublimely. Your eye for detail is unmatched. It shows in the clothes you make. Not everything works with each body type but every body type can find something that makes them look good. That's a skill. And a gift."

"Thank you," Hannah said. She couldn't decide if she was disappointed that his critique was limited to her wardrobe or happy that he'd listened to her when she'd asked him not to talk about her body. Talk about being confused. If she could, she'd blame her confusion on being tired, and while that was true, it didn't account for all of it. The truth was, she'd been mixed up ever since Russell had kissed her. Although she'd managed to function, that memory was never far from her mind.

"So, are you about ready to go?"

She laughed. "Forget everything I said about having a career in retail. You have so much to learn. Like about restocking and cleaning."

"You mean you don't have a service for that? Cleaning, not stocking."

"No. I actually have one full-time employee, Talia, and a high school girl, Alyssa, who works after school and on weekends. Unfortunately Talia called in sick again this morning and Alyssa has gone out of town with her family. In the past I was able to keep up on my own. Now I'm sinking. This season has been busier than I'd anticipated. Not that I'm ungrateful for the added business."

"Let's get to it, then."

"You don't have to stay. I know this isn't how you'd planned to spend your leave."

"Obviously you don't know a lot about pretend boyfriends, so let me give you the scoop. We don't ever leave our faux girlfriends to work while we play. It goes against everything we believe in. Just point me in the direction of the broom and I'll get to work."

"Alrighty, then." She showed him where she kept her cleaning supplies, then went up front and turned off the Christmas music.

"Man, that's cold. I realize that I'm not the greatest singer in the world, but I was in tune."

"What?"

"You turned off the music midsong. Right before I was about to hit that long, high note."

"Oh." Hannah actually hadn't been aware Russell was singing. She'd just been anxious to rid herself of the infernal carols. "Aren't you tired of Christmas music? We've been listening to these same songs for hours." *And hours.* "I thought it would be nice to listen to something besides songs about bells for a while."

"Songs about bells?"

"You know. Jingle bells. Silver bells, Carol of the bells, Christmas bells."

He looked at her quizzically, as if he were adding up clues that she hadn't realized she'd dropped and was close to coming up with an answer. Fortunately he let the matter drop. "I probably wasn't going to come anywhere near hitting that note anyway."

"Just to be on the safe side, I'll keep the music turned off. My ears could use a rest."

"Is that your not-too-subtle way of telling me not to talk to you?"

She sputtered. "No. Gosh no."

He laughed. "Pay no attention to me. I'm just giving you a hard time. Apparently I'm not as funny as I've been led to believe. People generally laugh when I'm around."

"With you or at you?"

He played invisible drums and hit the imaginary cymbal. "Ba-dum-bump. I know, you're here all week."

She nodded. "If we don't want to be here all night, we need to get back to work."

"Agreed."

Hannah began to neaten the shelves. She took off each item and folded it properly. If it was in need of steaming, which fortunately most were not, she added it to the pile on the counter to be taken care of later. As she worked, the stress of the day began to fade away and she began to relax. When she finished with the shelves, she began to work on the racks. In under an hour, she'd restocked everything and Russell had completely cleaned the store.

"You need help," Russell said as he folded the cloth he'd used to clean the mirrors and windows and then draped it over the top of the bottle of glass cleaner. "There's no way you can continue to run the store by yourself."

"You're right. Thankfully help is on the way. Alyssa, the high school girl I told you about, will be coming back tomorrow. I could still use a little more help, but I'll be able to breathe again."

"Does that mean you'll be able to take an hour off here or there? You know, for dating and stuff."

"Dating and *stuff*?"

He wiggled his eyebrows, looking positively devilish. "You know. Stuff."

"No, I don't know."

"Then I'll have to show you." He placed the cleaning supplies on the table beside the magazines and sauntered in her direction. His eyes were lit with mischief and his stride was filled with purpose as he closed the distance between them. She stood frozen until she realized that he was serious. Then her legs unlocked and, laughing, she made a dash for the relative safety of the changing rooms.

Before she had taken three steps, he'd passed her and was blocking her escape route.

She blinked and looked behind her. "How did you get in front of me? And how did you know where I was going?"

"I have skills."

"Or you were just lucky."

"Luck had nothing to do with it. It was all part of my master plan. I have you right where I want you."

"Where's that? Three feet from the changing rooms?"

"No." He pointed up and her eyes followed. "Under the mistletoe."

Sure enough the green-and-red plant was dangling from the ceiling, courtesy of Alyssa. Since Hannah hadn't been in the Christmas spirit and her capacity for faking went only so far, she'd given Alyssa free rein to decorate the boutique. Hannah had done her best to ignore the lights, wreaths and other assorted ornaments. Maybe if she'd paid more attention she would have spotted the mistletoe. Then she could have ripped it down and thrown it away. "I didn't put that there."

"That doesn't matter. We're still standing here. And unless we want to risk offending the Christmas spirits, we have to kiss. It's the law."

She couldn't give a flying fig about Christmas spirits. They'd abandoned her long ago. "Somehow I doubt Chief Knight is going to take us away in handcuffs if we don't."

Russell put his hands on her waist, holding her in place. "Not Sweet Briar law. The law of the Christmas spirits. You might be willing to risk getting on their bad side, but I'm not. The last thing I want is for them to rattle chains and show me every mistake I've ever made while I'm trying to sleep."

For the life of her, she couldn't think of a clever reply. Or any type of reply for that matter. Her heart began to pound with anticipation and her knees grew weak. As he lowered his head, bringing his lips within mere millimeters of hers, she closed her eyes. Her brain was scrambled and one thought repeated. *This is really going to happen.* They were going to kiss again. When his lips touched her cheek, she nearly groaned with agonized frustration. What about the rules of mistletoe? See, this was further proof that the Christmas spirits—whoever they were—had it in for her.

After pecking her cheek, Russell straightened. "That should satisfy them, don't you think?"

At least the Christmas spirits were satisfied, even if she wasn't. Russell seemed positively delighted with himself. Yay for him.

"Sure." How she managed to grit out the word with her teeth clenched tightly enough to crack her jaw she'd never know.

He removed one of his hands from her waist and rubbed his chin. He'd started the day clean-shaven, but nearly twelve hours later there was the hint of stubble along his jawline. "I don't know. Just to be on the safe side, I think we should give it another shot."

While she was trying to figure out what he meant, he bent his head to hers once more. This time his lips didn't come near her cheek, but instead they landed on hers. His mouth was firm, without the slightest hesitation or doubt that his kiss would be welcome. Ever so slowly he pulled her up against him. His muscular chest was just as hard as she'd imagined, and she ran her fingers over it before wrapping her arms around his neck.

She'd kissed her share of men in her lifetime, but none of them had made her feel what she was feeling now. It was as if she could fly. She was sure she would float into the air like a helium balloon if he released her. She could kiss him like this forever.

Unfortunately her phone rang, ensuring that she wouldn't be leaving the ground. But considering that this was only a fake relationship, it was probably for the best. The last thing she needed to do was set herself up to be hurt when he walked away. And regardless of how good his kisses felt or how much fun she'd had with him today, she knew he would leave. Why wouldn't he? They weren't committed to each other so he was under no obligation to stay. She was under no illusion that he would. After all, he'd left before.

With great reluctance, she pulled away and looked at her phone. It was a number she didn't recognize, but since she used the phone for business, she couldn't just ignore it. Turning away, more so she didn't have to look into Russell's gorgeous eyes than for a need of privacy, she answered the call.

She listened for a minute and smiled. It was a former employee of hers whose family had moved to Tennessee. Natasha was in town visiting her grandmother and wanted to pick up a few hours of work at the boutique. She was one of the best employees Hannah had ever had so she was quick to tell her yes. Natasha would start at nine the following morning.

After ending the call, Hannah let out a cheer. "Yes!"

"I take it that was good news."

"The best." She smiled.

"Your sister, mother and your ex have decided to leave town."

"Okay, maybe not the best news, but a close second. One of my former employees is in town and hoping to pick up a few hours of work."

He nodded. "I'm glad to hear it. No need to thank me."

She blinked. Had she heard him right? Maybe the kiss affected her hearing. "Why would I thank you?"

"Because I'm the one who insisted we kiss. We made the Christmas spirits happy and they rewarded us."

"I see. And just which Christmas spirits are these? I'm familiar with the Past, Present and Future ones. I'm not at all familiar with the spirit of mistletoe. In fact, from the little I know about mistletoe, it has very little to do with kissing."

"It didn't. Until the spirits got involved."

"Which ones?"

"Does it matter? There are a lot of Christmas spirits. Too many to name right now. I'll tell you more about them later. Right now, let's lock up and then go get some food."

"You realize that the diner is closed and there aren't any fast-food places in Sweet Briar."

"Who needs fast food when your brother owns the best restaurant in a three-state area? Three continents if you ask him."

"I thought you weren't going to let your family know you were here yet."

"I wasn't. But if we're going to be gallivanting around town, they'd find out anyway and be hurt that I hadn't let them know I was here. So I took a minute while I was steaming clothes and called Brandon. He's holding a table for us."

"Really? Let me run a comb through my hair."

"Your hair looks fine. You might want to fix your lipstick, though."

She blushed. "Right back atcha."

He swiped the back of his hand against his lips, effectively removing the traces of her ruby red lipstick.

Once she'd combed her hair and freshened her makeup, they locked the boutique and headed for Heaven on Earth, the restaurant owned by Russell's younger brother. Since the evening was pleasant for December, they walked the short distance.

The mayor and the town council really got into the spirit of decorating for the holidays. Ordinarily the large pots strategically placed on the sidewalks were overflowing with seasonal flowers. During the spring and summer months, they were bursting with reds, yellows and purples. The colors changed in the fall to oranges and golds. The business owners had gotten into the spirit and most, including Hannah, had added pots in front of their shops with similar flowers in them throughout the year.

But on the day after Thanksgiving, they'd put away the mums and pulled out the miniature spruce trees, poinsettias, holly and ivy and decorated them with multicolored bulbs. Unlike other towns that decorated exclusively with white lights, Sweet Briar used a variety of colors that even a newly minted scrooge like herself had to acknowledge looked good. The trunk on each tree lining the street was wrapped in green lights. The branches on the trees alternated between red and blue lights, giving the streets a festive appearance. All in all, Sweet Briar's business district looked a lot like Christmas. Sadly it was just a reminder of the Christmas wedding that hadn't happened. And no matter how merry it *looked*, it didn't *feel* like Christmas. She'd lost the Christmas spirit and didn't know how to get it back.

The downtown business owners had agreed to coordinate their decorations. Mabel, the owner of the eponymous diner on Main Street, chaired the committee in charge of planning the design. A kind woman under normal circumstances, she'd ruled her committee with an iron fist. Once the decorations were selected, she'd given everyone strict orders on how and when to place them. Since Hannah had agreed that having unified decorations would appeal to the eye and be good for business, she'd stuck to the plan.

Russell and Hannah reached the restaurant in under ten minutes. When they stepped inside, they were greeted by a smiling hostess who recognized Russell and immediately led them to their table.

"Brandon told me to let him know the second you arrived." She handed them their menus, then headed back to the kitchen to find Russell's brother.

Hannah leaned back in the comfortable chair, the remains of her exhaustion draining away. "This is a real treat for me. Thank you."

"The pleasure is all mine."

They were sitting there smiling at each other when all of a sudden she noticed Brandon beside their table. She had no idea how long he'd been standing there. Judging by the broad grin on his face, it had been a while. "I can always come back later if you want to be alone."

"Don't be silly," Russell said as he stood and grabbed his brother in a tight hug. Not the man version of a hug, which generally was just a couple of slaps on the back, but an honest-to-goodness hug that reflected the love between the brothers.

Brandon was tall and muscular like Russell, but that's where the resemblance ended. While Russell had shaved his head, Brandon wore his hair in waist-length locs that he'd pulled into a ponytail. Brandon was dressed in an immaculate tailored suit whereas Russell was wearing khakis and a pullover. They were both very handsome men, but while looking at Brandon did absolutely nothing for Hannah, the sight of Russell made her pulse race.

"It's good to see you," Brandon said, including Hannah in his greeting.

"You, too," Russell said.

"When did you get to town?"

"Yesterday."

Brandon raised an eyebrow. "So where are you staying? Joni would have told me if you were staying with her and Lex."

"I'm staying with Hannah."

Brandon paused, then smiled and nodded. "I see."

Hannah wondered just what it was that he saw.

There was no reason to lie to Brandon. She was about to spill the beans when Russell spoke.

"You know Hannah and I met this summer. We've been getting to know each other better."

He'd tiptoed up to the line between truth and a lie but hadn't crossed it.

Brandon grinned. "Glad to hear it. Clearly my brother has good taste in women. Your taste, Hannah, might be a little suspect."

Hannah laughed with the brothers. "I don't know. I'm pretty happy with my choice so far."

"Good enough." Brandon looked around the restaurant. Not a table was empty. "I'm going to mingle with my guests. Enjoy your dinner."

"Thanks."

After Brandon walked away, Hannah turned to Russell. "I feel bad that you have to lie to your family."

"Don't. It only makes sense. The fewer people who know a secret, the easier it is to keep it." Russell took a swallow of his water, then continued. "If we'd told him, he'd have to tell Arden. Brandon would never keep a secret from his wife. And then we'd have to tell Joni and Lex. This mission is classified. It's strictly need-to-know, and they don't. Besides, we don't want to put them in a position where they might have to cover for us."

"True." Hannah sighed. She wouldn't want her

friends to have to lie about her and Russell's fake relationship.

"And having them think we're involved also helps me. I still need time and space to figure out my next move without familial input. And since they believe we're involved neither Joni nor Brandon will pester me to stay with them and smother me with unwanted attention."

"So I'm helping you, too."

"More than you know. Now that Brandon and Joni have settled down and have families, my parents have turned their sights on me. My mother has started to talk about introducing me to a nice woman. I'm not interested in being fixed up with a woman, no matter how perfect my mother thinks she might be. Our relationship will help keep them off my back."

"They're in Chicago."

"Yes. But they're going to spend Christmas here. That's one of the reasons why I came to Sweet Briar instead of going home to Chicago. They want our entire family to celebrate the holidays together. Since Lex is the mayor and needs to be here for all the public events, they're coming to town."

"That sounds nice," Hannah said, struggling not to feel envious. It wasn't his fault that her family was such a disaster.

"It is. I've missed so many holidays and birthdays over the years. Too many to count. I'm look-ing forward to this Christmas season and all of the family gatherings." He patted her hand. "They'll be even more enjoyable with my new girlfriend by my side. The pressure will be off."

"You want me to go with you?" She wasn't sure how she felt about that. For the past couple of years, with a few exceptions, she'd managed to avoid the Christmas parties. She'd given gifts to her employees and hosted a small Christmas luncheon for them. She'd also exchanged Secret Santa gifts with her friends. But she'd begged off tree-trimming parties and shopping expeditions.

"Of course. It would be pretty strange to show up without my girlfriend."

"Just how many get-togethers are we talking about?"

He shrugged carelessly. In that moment, he looked carefree. Youthful. Not that thirty-eight was all that old. He was only five years older than she was. But he usually seemed to carry the weight of the world on his shoulders. Perhaps that came from being a soldier. Or maybe it stemmed from him being the oldest child. Whatever the reason, she found the more relaxed Russell just as appeal-ing as the intense one.

"I might not be able to attend them all," she said, feeling suddenly claustrophobic. The idea of being around his loving family appealed to her while simultaneously making her stomach churn with anxiety. That reaction was just plain silly. His siblings and their spouses were her friends. They'd been nothing but welcoming from the time she'd met each of them. Plus she'd met his parents briefly at Arden and Brandon's wedding and they'd been kind, as well. But still, she felt the need to create an escape route. "I have a lot to do at the boutique."

"I know. We'll attend as many functions as you're able."

She nodded.

He placed his hand on hers and gave it a gentle squeeze. Although she knew he'd simply been trying to put her at ease, her skin burned from the contact and electricity shot from her hand and darted throughout her body.

This was so not good. She wasn't supposed to be turned on by her fake boyfriend. But telling that to her body that was suddenly tingling with excitement didn't make a difference.

Oh, she was in trouble here.

Chapter Six

Russell reclined in his chair, watching as Hannah polished off her dessert. It had been a while since he'd enjoyed himself so much on a date. Not that this was a real date. They weren't actually a couple. He and Hannah were simply making the best of a strange situation. Not that being around her was a hardship. Far from it. She was sweet and intelligent with a great sense of humor. With all her charms it was no wonder he found himself becoming more attracted to her.

Hannah had been blessed with flawless brown skin, wavy black hair and the most beautiful face he'd ever seen. She could be on the cover of fashion magazines. And her body, with its sweet curves. *Whew!* But it wasn't the gorgeous face or sexy body that appealed the most to him. It was her kind heart and generous spirit that had attracted him from the first time he'd laid eyes on her and had only grown with each interaction.

"This has been nice," Hannah said. "I can't think of the last time I've had this much fun."

He could. He knew the exact date and time. It was the first night he and Hannah had spent together. They'd both been guests at a beach cookout Joni and Lex had hosted the night before he'd left to return to the base. Neither he nor Hannah had been interested in playing volleyball with the others, so they'd strolled along the sand, their shoes dangling from their fingers. The moonlit evening had been warm, and a cool breeze had blown, lifting Hannah's dark hair and blowing it around her face. She'd laughed as she'd pulled it away time after time before finally braiding it and pinning it on top of her head. He'd longed to undo that braid and tangle his hands in her hair. Thinking better of it, he'd kept walking. He hadn't wanted to move too fast. Back then he'd believed he'd had plenty of time to get to know her better.

He'd been wrong. That summer night had been all the time they'd been given. When he'd left, he'd intended to keep in touch. But he'd gotten injured a few days after he'd gotten back to his duty station. His hope and plans for the future had gone up in flames much like his Humvee. After he'd gotten the doctor's prognosis, he'd known he couldn't contact her. As much as he'd longed to hear her voice, he hadn't called her. He couldn't drag her into his suddenly messed-up life.

Yet when he'd arrived in Sweet Briar a few days ago, a week earlier than planned, she'd been the first person he'd thought of. The one person he'd yearned to see. It was as if his feet had minds of their own. He'd sought her out before he'd unpacked, something he would never do under ordinary circumstances.

But these weren't ordinary circumstances. Nothing in his life had been right since his injury. From the looks of things, it wouldn't go back to being normal for quite some time. If ever. Despite knowing that, he couldn't keep away from Hannah. It was as if an invisible cord bound them together and he was powerless to break free.

"I've enjoyed myself, too." He gestured for the waitress to bring their check even though he knew Brandon wouldn't accept a cent from him.

"Brandon said it's on the house," the waitress said, confirming what he'd already known.

"Thank you." Russell estimated the cost of the dinner and added it to the tip. He wished that she'd brought the check in a folder so that he could be more discreet.

The waitress looked at the bills he handed her and her eyes widened. "There's no charge."

"My hardheaded little brother's stubbornness is your gain. Besides, the service was excellent. Merry Christmas."

The waitress smiled broadly as it dawned on her that the money was her tip. "You, too. Both of you."

He pulled out Hannah's chair. When she stood, he gave in to temptation and placed a hand on the small of her back, guiding her through the maze of tables and chairs.

"That was nice of you," Hannah said once they were standing outside again.

"It was no big deal. It didn't cost me any more than dinner would have. But you know my brother. He won't take a penny from family."

"From what I hear, you helped him finance the restaurant."

"He had most of the money already. The little I gave him didn't make a difference." He searched for something else to discuss. The last thing he wanted to talk about was money. Family helped family. But then, having seen hers in all their unvarnished glory, one sibling helping another might be a foreign concept to her. She definitely needed to spend quality time with a loving family. Luckily his was available and as loving as they came.

They walked slowly back to the boutique, stopping now and then to speak with someone she knew or to window-shop.

A group of teenaged boys suddenly emerged from the pizza parlor, laughing and roughhousing. Russell stepped in front of Hannah while letting the teens pass. He put his foot wrong and his leg gave out, sending crippling pain through his body. Reaching out, he grabbed Hannah's arm, barely managing to stay upright. "Damn."

"Are you okay?"

"I'm fine." He yanked his hand back, trying to break the connection between them.

"Let's sit down a minute."

"I can walk." He knew he was being stubborn, but he hated the weakness. It came out of nowhere, striking him when he least expected it. Weeks could pass where he'd felt almost as strong as before. Then out of the blue, his leg would weaken. True, the incidents were fewer and farther between, just as the doctor had predicted, but they hadn't stopped completely.

Acting as though she hadn't heard him, Hannah grabbed his arm and steered him to an iron bench at the edge of the sidewalk. The weakness had already passed, and he was good to go, but when he inhaled Hannah's floral scent, he found himself walking docilely beside her to the bench.

Though it was getting late, the area was filled with merrymakers. Main Street had been blocked to traffic and four different Christmas displays had been erected in the intersection.

"That's so nice," he said, pointing at a scene of Santa's workshop. "It reminds me of when I was a child. Every year my parents took me, Joni and Brandon to downtown Chicago to see the department store windows. The larger stores had elaborate Christmas vignettes on display. The elves making toys in the North Pole was my favorite scene. I would have stood there all day."

Hannah barely glanced at where he'd pointed. "Yes."

"You're not much of a Christmas fan."

"What makes you say that?"

He noticed that she didn't deny it. Not that the holidays were for everyone. Truth be told, he hadn't done much celebrating these past years. Not because he disliked Christmas. He'd been away from home, so other than buying and shipping gifts for his family, the day had passed like so many others. But Hannah seemed to want to wish it away.

Of course, he could be reading more into her actions than was there. After all, he couldn't read her mind. But he didn't think he was wrong. Her store was decorated and Christmas music blared from the speakers, but despite those outward indications of Christmas joy, she didn't have the Christmas spirit.

"Just a wild guess."

"I guess I've outgrown some childish rituals. But that's part of growing up."

"Could be." He didn't for a moment think that was all of it, but he wasn't going to prolong the discussion when it was obvious it was making her uncomfortable. But he mentally expanded his mission. In addition to being her pretend boyfriend for the holidays, he would find a way to bring her some Christmas joy.

"How's your leg?"

"Fine." He stretched it out. "I can walk."

She stood and he did the same. He had the feeling that the earlier pleasure she'd felt at dinner had vanished with this conversation. But since his mood had taken a temporary turn for the worse when his leg had given way, he understood.

They didn't speak much on the walk back to their cars. After she got inside hers, she looked at him "See you at home."

He nodded. *Home.* It had a nice ring to it.

Hannah wanted to kick herself. Why had she made such a point of ignoring the Christmas displays when Russell had pointed them out? She should have made some banal comment or exclaimed in faked glee. Anything to hide the way she truly felt about the holiday. But no. She'd revealed her true feelings to Russell. He must think

she was a scrooge. And he'd be right. But that
didn't mean she wanted him to know. She didn't
want him to see her flaws. She wanted him to
think the best of her.

Why? She'd put her best foot forward this past
summer. But it hadn't been enough for him to call
her as he'd promised. So if he thought of her as a
Grinch, what did it matter? And why should she
have to fake her feelings anyway? She didn't have
to uphold an image for him or anyone else. The
years of pretending that the dirt her family did behind closed doors vanished once you stepped over
the threshold and into public view had somehow
crept back into her thoughts. Keeping up appearances had somehow become important again. She
pushed the urge away, determined not to pretend
to be something she wasn't.

Besides it was too late to worry about his opinion now. She pulled into her driveway, leaving
space for Russell to park beside her. The lights
were on a timer, so her house and bushes were illu-
minated by colorful lights. She stared at them for
a moment, seeing if they held any magic. Looking at them didn't create the slightest bit of joy
in her heart. Maybe she'd add the three-foot-tall
plastic candy canes and Nativity scene. Perhaps
that would do the trick. She doubted it.

They got out of their cars, climbed the stairs
and went into her house. Hannah enjoyed Rus-

sell's company, but she needed some time on her own. Who knew what would come spilling out of her mouth if she was alone with him much longer. Dinner had been like something out of a dream. Her dream. She'd fantasized about Russell for weeks after he'd gone back to his duty station. It was only after she'd realized that he wasn't going to call her that she'd begun to feel foolish. The feeling had been all too familiar and one she'd vowed never to feel again. It had taken a while, but she'd finally stopped thinking about him and hoping he'd call.

Now here he was, standing in her living room just as she'd once imagined. But it was no more real than her dreams had been. He wasn't her boyfriend. Nor was he interested in her. They were only pretending to care about each other until her family left town. Then he would be out of her life just like before.

"Well, I'm beat. I'm going to go to bed. Stay up as long as you like, Russell."

She turned to leave, but he grabbed her hand and spun her to face him. His dark eyes were seeking, searching her face for answers. "I feel as if I owe you an apology."

"For what?"

"Overstepping earlier."

"You didn't."

"I'd like for us to be friends."

"We are."

He nodded. "Good. Then I'll see you tomorrow."

She climbed the stairs. That had been the weirdest conversation. They'd been talking, but they hadn't really communicated.

Hannah brushed her teeth and then crossed the hall to her bedroom. She'd had some work done on the house since she'd moved in, but she hadn't created a master bathroom. Living alone, it hadn't been necessary. One bathroom had been enough for her. Now that she was sharing the house and bathroom with Russell, she wished she'd added a second bathroom instead of putting on a new roof. But he'd only be staying with her until her family left town. That was less than two weeks. Surely they could avoid any awkward situations for that long.

She found herself imagining Russell wrapped only in a towel, his torso glistening from the shower, and shoved the picture from her mind. That was just the type of situation she needed to avoid. Hannah hopped into bed and prayed for dreamless sleep. Tomorrow would be a long day.

Fortunately her prayers were answered and she felt refreshed when she awoke the next morning. She stepped into the hallway. As she reached the bathroom, the door swung open, revealing Russell wearing only a towel. Her mouth fell open and she could only stare. The reality of a nearly nude Russell was so much better than her imagination.

As she'd envisioned, his chest and shoulders were damp from the shower. But his body was so much more muscular than she'd imagined. His torso was perfectly sculpted with nary an ounce of fat. From his chest to his six-pack abs, he was an example of masculine excellence. There was a raised scar on his right shoulder and another one on his knee, but they didn't diminish his good looks. In fact, the scars gave him an air of danger. As her eyes feasted on the perfection before her, she could only imagine what secrets the terry cloth kept hidden.

Realizing she was staring, Hannah shook her head and forced her eyes back to his face. His dark eyes were filled with an intensity that made her quiver. She prayed that the desire burning through her didn't show on her face. "I'm sorry. I didn't know you were in here. I'll come back."

She turned to flee, but he grabbed her hand. The simple contact was almost her undoing. How could a calloused hand feel so good?

"I'm done here. If you'd shown up ten seconds later, I would have already been gone." His voice was huskier than she'd remembered. Raspier. Maybe because of the early hour.

"I got up extra early today so I could get a head start. It hadn't occurred to me that you might be an early riser." She realized she was babbling and forced her mouth closed.

"I had the same idea. Great minds think alike and all that." He took a step closer and she stepped out of the way. As he passed, she got a whiff of clean male mixed with aftershave, and she wobbled. She tried not to stare, but she couldn't help herself. He looked just as good from the back as he had from the front.

He turned to go into his room and she hastily looked away. But not before she'd seen the grin on his face. He'd caught her staring. Well, what did he expect? He might have the body of a god, but she was only human.

She stepped into the bathroom, closed the door and leaned against it. Her legs felt like goo and she needed the support. *What a man!* Hannah had never considered herself shallow, and had believed it was what was inside a man that mattered. Gerald hadn't liked working out and hadn't been especially muscular. Not that he'd been flabby. He'd just been...average. Of course, it turned out that his morals hadn't been anything special, either.

But Russell. He was sexiness personified. Over the past few months after he'd ghosted her, she'd begun to doubt the kind of man he was. Now she was beginning to wonder if her negative opinion of him could be wrong, leaving her confused. Was he the charming man he'd been during those wonderful summer hours they'd spent together? Or was he the indifferent man he'd been when he'd broken his word? Maybe both. Maybe neither. She didn't know. But the man he was now was pretty appealing and someone she'd like to know better.

She forced the rash thought away. It didn't matter who Russell Danielson turned out to be. He was only her pretend boyfriend. The love affair was make-believe. If she didn't want to end up with a real broken heart, she'd better not forget it.

Hannah showered quickly, using her favorite scented body wash. When she was done, she took off her shower cap, shook out her hair and then reached for a towel. Once she'd dried off, she followed up with scented lotion. She looked around the bathroom and sucked in a breath. She hadn't brought a robe. It hadn't occurred to her to grab the robe, hanging mostly unused, from the hook inside her closet door.

She mentally calculated the distance from the bathroom to her bedroom. She could make it in ten steps. Eight if she ran. But why would she run? Russell was probably in his room. Or better yet, in the kitchen brewing coffee and cooking another great breakfast for them to share. And really, what were the odds that she would step out of the bathroom wrapped only in a towel and run into him on the same day as he had run into her? Practically nil. She boldly grabbed the doorknob, gave it a firm turn, opened the door and stepped into the hallway. She looked around. Russell was nowhere to be seen. She couldn't decide if she was relieved or disappointed that she hadn't encountered him.

Her heart slowed as she walked to her room.

"Of course I'm relieved," she muttered to herself.

"Relieved about what?"

She shrieked and turned. Russell was standing at the top of the stairs. In a replay of twenty minutes ago with the roles reversed, his eyes traveled slowly over her body from head to toe. With each passing second, her body grew warmer and her skin tingled.

"Where did you come from?"

He pointed over his shoulder. "I cooked breakfast. I was just coming to let you know it was done. I heard the water stop running a while ago, so I figured you were already in your room and dressed. Lucky for me I forgot that women took longer to dry off then men."

"Uh."

He walked up the last step and closed the distance between them. He touched her shoulder. "You missed a spot."

The feel of his hand turned her skin to fire. He must have been burned too because he jerked his hand away.

"Thanks. I'll be right down."

He shook his head and after a brief hesitation turned and walked back downstairs.

Hannah watched him go as if frozen in place. Then she gave herself a mental slap and walked the last two steps to her room. When she was inside, she heaved a heavy sigh. What in the world was wrong with her? As if trying to recapture the moment, she touched her shoulder where only moments ago Russell's hand had caressed that skin. "Silly girl," she whispered and then turned around to make sure Russell hadn't somehow heard that, too.

She dressed carefully in one of her favorite designs, a blue-and-purple floral dress with a hot pink belt, and then went downstairs. Russell was standing beside her fireplace, staring out the window.

"What's so interesting?" she asked, going to stand beside him.

"Oh, nothing. I was just getting a feel for the neighborhood."

"My house still isn't for sale," she joked.

He laughed, then, turning, grabbed her hand as if it were the most natural thing in the world to do. "I guess I'll have to persuade you to take me in as a boarder."

She led him into the kitchen. "If breakfast tastes as good as it smells, I might just do that."

"Now the pressure is really on."

Hannah laughed as she filled her plate.

They enjoyed breakfast, the uncomfortable

towel incidents momentarily forgotten. They'd just finished eating when Hannah's doorbell rang. She blew out an exasperated sigh. "That had better not be my sister."

"Does she have your address?"

"I certainly didn't give it to her. But this is a small town. It wouldn't be hard to find me."

"I'll get it. And if it's your sister, I'll get rid of her." Russell was out of the room in the blink of an eye.

Hannah fought back the feeling of delight that filled her. She might not need him or any other man to fight her battles, but it felt good knowing that he would. Still, her family was her problem and she would be the one to deal with them. Standing, she followed him through the house. She reached the front room just as he opened the door.

"What are you doing here?" she heard him asking.

"I came to see my brother and his girlfriend."

Joni. Hannah sighed. Russell's sister showing up unexpectedly meant Hannah would have to lie to one of her dearest friends today. This relationship was taking on a life of its own.

Chapter Seven

Hannah smiled as she watched her good friend hug Russell, happy to see the reunion between brother and sister. When Joni spotted her, she grinned. "You've got some explaining to do."

Hannah laughed. "Whatever do you mean?"

"Don't play the innocent with me. Why didn't you tell me you're dating Russell? I had to hear it from Brandon. And when I asked him about it all he would say is that you'd eaten dinner at Heaven on Earth last night. You know how Brandon is. He didn't give me any details."

"What kind of details do you want?" Russell asked, coming to stand beside Hannah and wrapping an arm around her waist. Despite knowing he was just putting on a show for Joni—after all, he needed to convince his family they were dating, too—her toes curled at the contact. Russell might not know it, but his touch was lethal and had the power to make her forget that this whole relationship was pretend.

"None from you," she said. "It's just as hard to pry information from you as from Brandon." Joni turned back to Hannah. "How long have you been seeing each other? And why didn't you tell me?"

"Not long," Hannah said.

"Since this summer," Russell said at the same time.

"We spent time together when Russell was here visiting this summer," Hannah clarified. "When he got back to town, he stopped in to see me."

"I see." Joni grinned. "A week before he told anyone he would be here. I have a feeling that you're leaving out quite a bit, but I'll let it slide for now. I don't want to overstay my welcome. Besides, I have to get home and pick up the baby so Lex and I can get to work. I just wanted to say hello and give my brother a kiss. And to invite you to dinner. Are you free tonight?"

"Not if you're cooking," Russell quipped.

"Don't be silly. Lex handles all that. And Joshua would love to see his uncle Russell." Joni and Lex had an adorable one-year-old son.

Russell looked at Hannah as if seeking her agreement before responding. She nodded. Although she would have rather spent time alone with Russell, given the increased level of sexual attraction she felt, it was probably best that they didn't spend too much time alone. Who knew what would happen between them?

"We'll see you tonight."

"Okay. I'll let Lex know."

"Joni," Russell said as his sister turned to leave.

"Yes?"

"Have you told Mom and Dad that I'm here?"

She shook her head.

"Good. Don't. I don't want them rushing down to see me. Especially when they'll be here in a few days anyway."

Joni smiled. "Not to mention that they'll interrupt your alone time with Hannah. My lips are sealed. See you tonight."

Once Joni had left, Hannah grabbed her purse and turned to say goodbye to Russell. She was surprised to see that he was grabbing his jacket.

"I thought I'd help you out again today."

"You don't have to help me out every day."

He flashed her the grin that she was growing used to seeing. From the way her heart jumped, she clearly wasn't immune to him. "I like being around you."

Warning herself not to read too much into his words, she walked beside him to their cars.

"Do you mind if I ride in with you?"

"Sure. But what if you want to leave early?"

"I won't. But this is a small town. I can easily jog over and get my car."

She didn't mention the weakness in his leg. If he had somewhere to go, she'd offer him her car.

As they drove down the quiet streets, she couldn't keep from glancing at him. Dressed in a long-sleeve gray shirt and black jeans, he looked so handsome it was hard not to stare. She could only imagine how devastating he'd look in his dress uniform. Lucky for her, there wasn't a reason for him to wear it here. If she saw him in it, she might not be able to restrain herself. The last thing either of them needed was for her to throw herself at him.

"You don't mind having dinner with my sister, do you?" he asked.

"Of course not. I love Joni. I'd trade her for my sister any day."

He laughed. "I bet you would. I'm going to have to say no."

"I didn't think you'd go for that."

He sobered. "Have you heard from any of them?"

"Mercifully no. Maybe they went back home. Or better yet, maybe they went for a walk and stepped in quicksand."

"Is there a lot of quicksand in the area?" His voice was filled with amusement.

"Not that I know of, but a girl can hope."

She parked in front of the boutique. As she was unlocking the door, she heard her name being called. She looked over her shoulder and spotted her sister and mother. Luckily Gerald was nowhere to be seen.

"Looks like we talked them up," Russell said.

"Where's quicksand when you need it?"

"I can run interference if you want."

She shook her head. "It's tempting, but no. My family, my problem."

Russell nodded in approval and her heart warmed. She shoved the reaction away. She didn't need his approval. The need for approval was why she was in this mess.

Hannah stood outside the shop waiting for Dinah and Eleanor to reach her. Although she didn't want to air her dirty laundry in public, it was preferable to letting them inside the boutique.

"What do you want?" Hannah wasn't ordinarily rude, but she was no longer going to try to win the love of people who clearly didn't love her. And she was done giving respect only to receive disrespect in return.

"To talk," Dinah said, putting on her most persuasive smile. Apparently she was back pretending that they had a close relationship. "Surely we can do that."

"What could we possibly have to discuss?"

"Is that any way to talk to your sister?" Eleanor chided. "We're family and should act like it."

"You first," Hannah muttered.

Eleanor sighed, playing the role of the ever-put-upon mother, then turned to Russell. "You seem like a good man. You have parents and a brother and sister. Could you ever imagine talking to them this way?"

Russell shook his head. "No, I couldn't."

Eleanor and Dinah shared triumphant grins and Hannah felt her heart sink a little at his betrayal.

"But then," Russell continued, "I can't imagine sleeping with my brother's fiancée. And I know for damn sure that neither of my parents would condone such behavior if I did."

Eleanor's smile faded and she sputtered as she searched for a comeback. Dinah looked like she'd swallowed a worm.

"If there's nothing else, I need to get to work," Hannah said.

"I need you to design my dress," Dinah said.

Hannah blew out an aggravated breath. "Why? Really, why in the world do you want me to design your dress? I could make you something that made you look like a clown."

"Because you're famous and I'm your sister."

"One, I'm not famous," Hannah said, counting on her fingers for emphasis, "and two, we're not sisters in the true sense of the word. Blood doesn't make family." Hannah included her mother in that remark.

"But," Dinah stammered.

"You may as well go home. I am not now, nor will I be in the future, designing anything for you." Hannah enunciated each word.

"Let's go inside," Eleanor urged. "I raised you better than to conduct family business where it could be overheard."

"No, Mother," Dinah countered. "Let's stay out here. Let people know the kind of person Hannah really is. Everybody we met thinks you're so wonderful. So talented. But that's because they don't know how you treat your family."

Hannah's heart stopped at the idea of creating a scene, but the smirk on Dinah's face made her rash. "Go right ahead. These people are my friends. They've known me for years. But you? They don't know you from Adam. As you said, I'm famous. Maybe I'll call a few reporters I know and tell them how I walked in on my sister and my former fiancé in bed a week before my wedding. How do you think the high-society people you yearn to rub elbows with will look at you?"

"You wouldn't."

"Try me."

Hannah faced down her sister. She had no intention of spilling the private details of her dysfunctional family to anyone. She hadn't even told her closest friends why she'd decided to move here. The pain and embarrassment had been too overwhelming. And she certainly didn't want strangers to know the dirty details of her relationship with her mother and only sibling. But Dinah didn't know that. Since Dinah and Eleanor weren't above blackmail, they just assumed she was just as unethical and vicious as they were.

"Perhaps we'll come back at another time," Eleanor said, pulling Dinah away. Hannah knew her mother well enough to know this wasn't the end. She was simply going to regroup and come up with another plan since the direct way wasn't working.

Hannah watched as her family—and that was using the word loosely—stalked down the street and climbed into their car. She waited until they'd driven out of sight before moving.

Without saying a word, Russell took the keys from her and unlocked the door. Shaking herself out of her funk, Hannah quickly turned off the alarm and turned on the overhead lights. Russell switched on the Christmas lights and the tree. Seconds later the silence was replaced with Christmas music. Great. Just what she didn't need. More reminders of a painful Christmas season. As if her mother and Dinah's presence hadn't been enough to dredge up the memories.

Russell watched Hannah, unsure of how to make things better. Sadly, short of giving her a new family, there was nothing he could do. Acknowledging that made him feel incompetent—something he hated. It was bad enough that he was no longer capable of performing his job in the military. But being unable to take the pained expression from Hannah's face was ten times worse. He wished he had the power to make Hannah smile.

But he didn't. She needed a Christmas miracle. He had to find a way to make one happen.

Hannah walked around the store, making sure that everything was in order. Of course it was. She'd made sure of that before they'd left last night. But he had a feeling that following her routine was comforting to her, helping her to get her life back in balance.

Excusing himself, he went into the break room and made a pot of coffee. They'd each had a cup with breakfast, but he needed to do something constructive.

The bell over the front door tinkled as he was returning to the front of the shop. Hannah looked up and smiled as a young woman entered.

"Natasha. It's so good to see you," Hannah exclaimed as they embraced. "I really need the help."

The girl grinned. "I'm glad, because I can really use the money."

Hannah motioned for him to join them. "Russell, this is Natasha. She's the first employee I hired. She and her family recently moved away but she's spending the Christmas holidays in Sweet Briar with her grandmother. Natasha, this is Russell Danielson."

"Joni's brother?" she asked.

"Yes," he confirmed. "And Hannah's boyfriend."

Natasha's grin broadened. Apparently he met with her approval. "Nice to meet you."

"Likewise."

Natasha excused herself to put her belongings away, leaving Hannah and Russell alone. She touched his arm. "I have help now, so if you want to leave, you can."

"Are you upset with me for telling her I'm your boyfriend?"

Her eyes widened and then she looked away. "No. Of course not."

"Then why are you trying to get rid of me?"

"It's just…"

He put a finger under her chin and lifted her face until they were looking at each other. "Just what?"

"I'm embarrassed that you saw the scene with

my mother and Dinah. That's the second time in three days."

He caressed her cheek. "Don't be embarrassed. You're not responsible for their behavior."

"I don't want you to start looking at me differently."

"That won't happen. If anything, I admire you even more. You're a wonderful person who has endured the unimaginable. You should be able to rely on your family to support you, not have to protect yourself from them."

She nodded, but the sorrow remained in her eyes. He wished he could run her family out of town, but he obviously couldn't do that. Still, he intended to do everything in his power to keep them from hurting Hannah.

The clock chimed the hour and Hannah unlocked the front door and flipped the sign from Closed to Open. Minutes later a few women entered the boutique, the beginning of a steady stream of shoppers who flowed through the store all day. Another employee, a high school girl named Alyssa, arrived in the afternoon to help, giving Hannah the opportunity to take a break.

Russell spent the day carrying boxes, steaming garments and doing whatever tasks needed doing in order to keep the shelves and racks stocked. He'd worked hard as a soldier, but his days spent recuperating had led to a lot of inactivity. He was happy to be doing something physical again.

When the last customer had left the shop, the boutique was nearly in order. With two additional people helping, they had the store cleaned and ready to reopen in the morning in no time flat. He and Hannah waited until Natasha had driven off and Alyssa's father had picked her up before heading to Lex and Joni's for dinner.

His sister's family lived in a four-bedroom house on a two-acre lot. Although Lex's family had made a fortune in the cosmetic and perfume business, Lex had resigned his position with the company and moved to Sweet Briar years ago and had run for mayor. Lex and Joni had been good friends for years, so Russell had been surprised when Joni had told him that she was pregnant and engaged to marry her old friend. It was clear that they were very much in love and happy together.

The same could be said for his brother, Brandon, and his wife, Arden. After a near fatal ending to a bad relationship, Brandon had left Chicago and started over in Sweet Briar. He'd met and married Arden, the love of his life, here. Russell was pleased that his siblings had found happiness and that their lives were on track.

He was at an age when he thought his life would be settled, as well. Instead his career was being snatched away from him. He had no idea where he was going professionally. He couldn't make a move because he had no direction. And he didn't know which way to go. And on the personal front, though he'd always believed he'd have plenty of time to find the right woman, his romantic life was nothing to write home about, either. Could it get any lower than needing a pretend girlfriend for the holidays?

Not that there was anything wrong with Hannah. Far from it. All day, he'd caught himself staring at her. She had the sexiest body he'd ever seen. At about five foot seven, she was just the right height for him. At six one, he wasn't attracted to short women. He liked being able to look his woman in the eyes when he was talking to her. When Hannah wore heels, they stood eye to eye. Mouth to mouth.

Today she was wearing a blue-and-purple dress that hugged her curvaceous body in a way that had him longing to do the same. The heady perfume she wore gave him ideas that he shouldn't be having about a pretend girlfriend. They'd been alone in the storeroom a couple of times, and the only thing that kept him from pouncing on her was the knowledge that they weren't truly alone. One of her employees could have walked in on them at any moment. That and the fact that he didn't want to shock or offend her.

He'd already crossed the line by kissing her that

first day. The minute she'd kicked her family out
of the shop, she'd reeled on him in anger. Not that
he blamed her. He hadn't had permission to kiss
her. So despite how much harder it was to remember their relationship was fake and the fact that his
attraction was growing by leaps and bounds, he
was going to exercise self-control from now on.
Of course, that was easier said than done.

Especially since the towel incident.

He wiped a hand across his suddenly damp
forehead. In all of his thirty-eight years, he'd never
seen anything sexier than Hannah wrapped in that
towel. That image would forever be emblazoned
in his mind. Her gorgeous brown skin had glowed
as if there was fire inside her. And perhaps there
was. Her skin had felt hot when he'd given in to
the temptation to touch her bare shoulder. He'd
practically scorched his skin and it had taken
every ounce of self-discipline he'd honed during
his years in the military to not unwrap that towel
and go from being fake lovers to lovers in reality.

But that wasn't what she'd signed up for. And
it certainly wasn't what she needed. Not after the
way her former fiancé had proved himself inca-
pable of keeping his word. Russell refused to be
anything like that selfish jerk. Russell had promised that Hannah would be safe with him living
in her house. He'd said that theirs would be a romance in name only and he intended to keep that

promise. So no matter how much he'd yearned for Hannah this morning, he'd forced his desires down and returned to the kitchen. He'd given his word and his word was his bond.

When they reached Joni's house, Hannah parked, and they walked to the front door. He grabbed her hand and she looked at him, a question in her eyes.

"We're supposed to be involved, remember?"

"True. But Joni and Lex are my friends. And they're your sister and brother-in-law. Do you really think we'll be able to fool them? Or that we need to?"

"Yes."

"To which question?"

"Both."

"I don't understand, but okay. They're your family."

"You make a good point. Joni is your good friend and my sister. It's going to take a lot to convince her. Maybe words aren't enough."

He tugged her hand, bringing her closer to him. He took a step in her direction and his body brushed against her softer one. Their eyes held. He could tell the minute she read the intent in his eyes and he paused, giving her a chance to object, praying hard that she wouldn't. She reached out and caressed his jaw.

Taking that gesture as consent, he brushed his

lips against hers in a gentle kiss. When he felt her respond, he wrapped his arms around her waist and deepened the kiss. She tasted like heaven.

The annoying sound of a throat loudly being cleared interrupted them and he reluctantly pulled back. Breathing hard, he leaned his forehead against Hannah's, unwilling to break all physical contact.

"Are you guys coming inside or are you going to make out in front of my house all night?" Joni asked. Her voice rang with amusement and Russell knew there would be a lot of razzing in his near future.

"Little sisters can be so pesky," Russell said, making sure that his voice carried.

"I heard that," Joni said, laughing.

"I meant for you to." He took Hannah's hand. It trembled in his.

He and Joni kept up a steady stream of banter as they stepped inside the house. He'd spent so much time away from his family that he'd forgotten just how much he liked them and enjoyed their company. Or maybe he appreciated their relationship more now that he'd been exposed to Hannah's family and realized just how lucky he'd been.

"Hi," Lex said, coming into the room, his one-year-old son in his arms. Joshua spotted a toy and squirmed and pushed against Lex's chest as he fought to get down. When Lex set him on the floor, he toddled to a plastic truck and dropped onto his diapered bottom.

"He's walking already?" Russell asked.

"Oh yeah. He's even climbing the stairs, hence the gate," Joni said.

"Where did the time go?" Russell asked, more to himself than to anyone else. It seemed like only yesterday Joni had sent him pictures of her newborn son. Joshua had been wrapped in a blanket, his eyes closed in peaceful sleep. Joni regularly sent pictures and videos of his nephew. Though they were nice, they didn't quite make up for not being there.

Hannah gave him a soft smile and squeezed his hand. Although he hadn't said a word, she understood his feelings.

"Time and dinner wait for no man," Joni said, scooping up her son and kissing his chubby cheeks. "Wash your hands so we can eat. The powder room is through there."

"How's the mayor business going?" Russell asked Lex a few minutes later when they were seated and dining on roast beef, twice-baked potatoes and asparagus.

Lex smiled. "It couldn't be better. We've had some challenging times as has much of the country, but our people pulled together, helping out wherever there was a need and making sure that no one went without. I've never been prouder of my town than I've been this past year. We're on track to having a very successful Christmas season. Tourists are flocking to town in numbers we haven't seen in a December before. Of course, a lot of that is due to the popularity of our resident designer to the stars."

Hannah blushed. "No. I think it has less to do with me and more to do with the programs you've put in place. You and Charlotte have come up with some tremendous ideas to attract people."

"Who is Charlotte?" Russell asked.

"Charlotte Shields-Tyler," Joni said. "She works for Lex. She's a genius at marketing and coming up with innovative ideas to draw businesses as well as tourists to town. The Christmas scenes on Main Street were her idea."

"She's done a terrific job. This whole town looks and feels like the North Pole."

Lex and Joni agreed. Russell noticed that Hannah had grown quiet during the conversation. Suddenly she seemed melancholy. It was as if the entire discussion made her uncomfortable and unhappy. Perhaps she was still feeling blue from the encounter she'd had with her family earlier.

"We're going to have a massive Christmas party for the kids at the youth center. With Santa and lots of elves and, of course, Christmas presents," Joni said.

"That sounds good. When?"

"December 22."

"Do you need any volunteers? I'd love to help." He'd missed so many Christmases with his family that he was going to make the most of this one.

Joni and Lex exchanged glances before Lex spoke. "As a matter of fact, we could use someone to play Santa. I was going to do it, but it would be better if you do it. Lots of kids in town know me and might recognize me even if I wore a costume. Most of them have never seen you, so there's little chance of them recognizing you."

"What would I have to do?"

"The usual Santa things. Hold kids on your lap and take pictures. And give out gifts."

"I can do that. It sounds like a lot of fun." He swallowed some water before continuing. "And you know, I think he could use a Mrs. Claus. What do you say, Hannah? Care to be my Mrs. for a night?"

Chapter Eight

Hannah felt three sets of eyes staring at her and her face started to burn. Did Russell just ask her to be Mrs. Claus at the town Christmas party? No way. The event had been well publicized in Sweet Briar and the neighboring ranches. She'd even hung a poster advertising the party in a window of the boutique. A bunch of fliers were stacked on the counter beside her cash register and she included one with each sale. She had no problem promoting the event, but she had no intention of going. Not only was it a Christmas party, it was going to be held on December 22. That was the date of her doomed wedding. She'd intended to work that day and then hole up in her house, counting the minutes until the clock struck midnight.

"No. Thanks for asking."

"Come on, it'll be fun," Russell cajoled, flashing a devastating smile that could have had her agreeing to anything. Except this. "The kids will love it."

"No." She replied a little more sharply than she'd intended, but dressing up as Mrs. Claus was out of the question. She barely managed to fake Christmas cheer as it was. There was no way she could find the strength to play Santa's wife for the entire town, even for a little while.

"How about dessert?" Joni said, before the moment could become any more uncomfortable. "I picked up a lemon meringue pie at the bakery."

"I guess I could choke down a slice or two of my favorite pie," Russell said as if the awkward moment had never occurred. If he'd been offended by her attitude, it didn't show. He was his normal, calm self.

Lex grabbed the empty dinner plates, waving away offers of help, and followed Joni from the room.

"I'm sorry," Hannah said to Russell. He might be willing to let the matter pass, but she couldn't act as if she hadn't behaved poorly.

"For what? You don't want to be Mrs. Claus.

I shouldn't have put you on the spot like that. If anyone should apologize, it's me. I'm sorry."

"Do you mean that?" Hannah's breath stalled in her throat as she awaited his response.

"Yes. So let's forget it."

Hannah smiled as the tension fled from her body.

Joni returned with the pie and Lex followed behind with dessert plates and spoons.

"Where's yours?" Russell asked with a wink. "There's only enough for me."

Lex groaned.

Joni laughed. "Told you. I know my brother."

Lex pointed at Russell. "I just lost a bet. Joni said you were going to say that. Now I have to clean the kitchen. Alone."

"Sorry to hear that," Russell said, clearly unbothered, "but that doesn't explain where the rest of the dessert is. I need to put on some pounds if I'm going to play Santa."

"The costume comes with padding," Lex said. "One slice per customer."

"He's kidding. There's another pie in the kitchen," Joni said, setting generous slices in front of them.

"That's better," Russell said, grinning.

The rest of the evening passed in a blur of laughter. Hannah wished that she and her sister could share the close relationship that Russell and his siblings shared. Hannah had made many overtures in the past, and forgiven many offenses, both great and small, before accepting the sad truth. Dinah wasn't interested in a relationship that didn't benefit her without her having to do any giving. Hannah and Dinah could never be sisters in the true sense of the word.

They lingered over dessert and coffee before saying their goodbyes. Hannah and Russell drove back to her house, talking quietly about the fun they'd had. He'd been staying with her for only a couple of days, so she couldn't claim to have gotten used to having him around. But she'd grown comfortable with his presence. He was good company and she wasn't lonely.

"How about a nightcap?" Russell asked as they stepped inside.

"You just want another piece of pie," Hannah joked, unbuttoning her coat. Russell was instantly beside her. She shrugged out of her coat and he hung it on the hook beside his jacket.

"I wouldn't mind."

She grinned. "Neither would I."

"If you'll serve, I'll get a fire going."

"Sounds good."

She went into the kitchen and put two slices of pie on dessert plates. After a brief hesitation, she grabbed a bottle of wine and a couple of glasses. When she returned to the living room, Russell had started the fire. He'd moved the two comfortable chairs that normally sat in front of the fireplace and had piled pillows on the floor, creating a cozy sitting area.

"Let me help you with that."

"Thanks. This looks comfortable," she said, taking a seat on a cushion.

"I thought this would be a nice change of pace."

With firelight providing the only illumination, the atmosphere was at once cozy and romantic. She hadn't anticipated an evening like this when they'd agreed to have a pretend romance. It probably wasn't wise to blur the line separating fantasy from reality, but she didn't have the desire to bring a halt to the evening just yet. Besides, this was a perfect opportunity to get to know each other better.

They'd started down that path that summer. She'd had such high hopes for their relationship. Everything had been wonderful. For the first time in a long while, she'd felt like she'd met a man she could picture becoming a part of her life. Sadly the romance she'd hoped for hadn't materialized. But that didn't mean they couldn't become friends.

He poured two glasses of wine, handing her one and keeping the other. Once they were comfortably settled, their legs stretched in front of them, they stared into the flickering firelight. They sat in silence for a while, the only sound coming when the burning logs popped periodically.

"Can I ask you a question?" Russell's voice was soft and she knew if she told him no, he wouldn't push it.

"Sure. But I don't promise to answer."

"That's fair." He swirled the wine in his glass, the red liquid changing colors as it caught the flames. Hannah was beginning to wonder if he'd changed his mind when he turned to look at her. His eyes were dark and she saw the question there.

"What's with you and Christmas? You don't seem to have the Christmas spirit."

"What do you mean?" she asked, trying to decide just how much she would reveal. She didn't feel compelled to bare her soul to him right now. They weren't that close yet. "Look around. I have lights outside and at the boutique. I play Christmas music from the moment the store opens until it closes. To me, that screams Christmas spirit."

He swallowed more wine then looked at her. Was that sympathy she saw in his eyes? Sympathy was the last thing she wanted from him. Or anyone. But apparently he could see through what she'd said to the truth she'd left unspoken. Hadn't she just thought that she wanted to be friends? Friends were honest with each other. Even so, she was under no obligation to reveal her pain so he could inspect it. Heck, she didn't even take it out so she could look at it herself. Once she'd ended her relationships with Gerald and her sister, she'd bottled up all the hurt, betrayal and disappointment she'd felt and hid it in a tiny part of her heart, never to look at it again. She was afraid that if she did, the pain would overwhelm her and she wouldn't be able to get over it.

"That's all external. Not to say that your house isn't beautifully decorated. It is. But the minute you walk inside your front door, it's like Christmas fails to exist. It could be any time of the year. And not simply because you don't have any decorations inside. The emotions are also missing. The atmosphere is so different. If I'm wrong or if I've overstepped, I apologize. But I'm your friend. I just want you to know that I care. I feel as if there is something wrong. Something hurting you. If there is anything I can do to help, just say the word."

Hannah stared at the fire, watching as the flames licked the wood. She had a decision to make. She could take the out he'd given her. Or she could open up. And really, what would it hurt to tell him? She'd kept the truth hidden, yet it hadn't stopped her from recalling the horrible day she'd caught Dinah and Gerald together. Nor had it kept her from thinking about the wedding that hadn't happened. Hiding hadn't changed a thing.

When she'd moved to Sweet Briar, she'd told

herself that she'd left Gerald and all that happened between them behind her. She'd cut him out of her life completely. She hadn't wanted to bring the memory of him into her future. Yet he'd physically come to Sweet Briar, barging into her shop and into the life she'd created here. And now she was about to talk about him. Would she never be rid of him?

"I was supposed to get married on December 22, three years ago. As you already know, I caught my sister in bed with my fiancé a week before that. So instead of going to my final dress fitting and enjoying the excitement leading up to my big day, I was calling guests to let them know the wedding was off and canceling venues and caterers. I spent what was supposed to be my wedding day in my room crying.

"To make matters worse, my sister wasn't the least bit repentant. Far from it. Not that I'd expected her to be at that point. But even so, I was surprised by her behavior. She acted as if she hadn't done anything wrong. In fact, she seemed proud of herself.

"My mother wasn't the least bit sympathetic. Most mothers would try to comfort their hurting child, but not mine." She paused, trying to push down the pain. Her vision blurred as her eyes filled with unshed tears. She squeezed her eyes shut, refusing to let even one drop fall. This was why she held her emotions captive. If she didn't, they would overwhelm her. Russell must have sensed her struggle because he didn't move or speak, letting her regain control of her emotions.

When she was sure she could talk without her voice revealing her pain, she continued. "Gerald and I were supposed to go on a ten-day cruise for our honeymoon. Obviously that didn't happen. You can guess who went with him in my place. Dinah. Do you know who dropped them off at the airport? My mother."

He rocked back, clearly appalled. "Oh. Wow. I have no words."

"Yeah. I've lived with it for three years and I'm still speechless myself."

"I can see why you might not want to celebrate the season."

She nodded.

They sat quietly for a minute. She imagined he was trying to process everything.

"Let's do something fun tomorrow," he said, leaning forward. "It doesn't have to be Christmas-related."

"Sounds good," she said, glad that he hadn't pressed her for more details. More than that, she was grateful that he hadn't told her to get over it and move on with her life as if she hadn't tried. "What do you have in mind?"

"I have no idea. I'll ask Joni for suggestions."

"I have to put in a few hours at the store. Fortunately all three of my employees will be working. We close early on Saturdays, so I shouldn't be tired."

"Great. I'll have firm plans by then."

She stretched and covered a yawn. "I guess I'd better get to bed. The wine has made me drowsy."

They both reached for the dirty dishes and their hands brushed. His face was mere inches away from hers. The warmth from his body wrapped around hers, rivaling the heat from the fire. The air crackled with sexual tension and her breathing became shallow. Unable to stop herself, she caressed his jaw and then kissed his lips. He tasted slightly of the lemon pie and the wine they'd consumed.

He put his arm around her waist and pulled her closer to him. He deepened the kiss and her longing for him grew. Then abruptly he jerked away from her and stood. Her eyes flew open and her pleasure vanished, rapidly replaced by chilly embarrassment.

What was wrong with her? Hadn't she walked down this rocky road before? First with Gerald, and then to a lesser degree this past summer with Russell. She should know better than to throw herself at a man who didn't want a romantic relationship with her. Russell had made it clear that he wasn't interested in her as a woman. Just thirty minutes ago he'd called her his friend. Heck, he hadn't even referred to her as his fake girlfriend. But then since they were alone in her house and there was no one there to see them, there was no need to pretend.

She recalled the look she'd seen in his eyes earlier. *Sympathy.* That was mere centimeters away from pity. That was even before she'd given him all the painful details of her last relationship. Before she'd told him how badly her mother had let her down. He'd understood the pain the rejection had caused and how this season brought it all back. Russell was a kind man. No doubt he'd returned her kiss to lessen the blow of his rejection. No matter how gently he'd done it, it still stung.

But she couldn't let him know that she was attracted to him. The last thing she wanted was to turn his sympathy to pity. They needed to pretend to be involved for only a few more days. Surely she could hold herself in check for that long.

"Sorry," she said, getting to her feet, as well. "I must have drunk more wine than I thought. I generally don't go around pouncing on my friends."

He rubbed the back of his neck and flashed her a sexy grin that had her wishing he was attracted to her. "I had a feeling it was something like that. Don't give it a second thought, okay? Why don't you go on up to bed. I'll take care of the dishes and setting this room back in order."

"Okay." She noticed the way he kept his distance from her. He'd shoved his hands in his pockets and was standing near the window. Swallowing her pain and humiliation, she turned and walked upstairs with as much dignity as she could muster. When she reached the sanctuary of her bedroom, she closed the door and flung herself on the bed. What had started out as a wonderful day filled with fun and laughter had turned into an embarrassing disaster.

But then, wasn't that always the way it went for her?

Russell waited until he heard Hannah's bedroom door close before allowing himself to move. Then blowing out a ragged breath, he sank to the floor. *Wow.* That kiss had practically burned him from the inside out. Even now, desire still raged inside him and it took every ounce of strength in his body not to climb the stairs, pound on Hannah's door and beg her to let him in. But he couldn't do that.

He'd barely managed to control himself this time. He'd come close to laying Hannah down on the pillows and making love to her. But then he'd spotted the empty wine bottle. Although she hadn't drunk all that much, he didn't know how it affected her. Her words only confirmed his thoughts. *I must have drunk more wine than I thought*. Obviously she wasn't in a place to consent. And he wasn't the type of man to take advantage of a woman.

Besides, starting a physical relationship right now would be a mistake—one they might not recover from. Their romance wasn't real. More important, their friendship was too new—too fragile—to survive that type of misstep. They needed to build their friendship before trying to have any other type of relationship.

Hannah was still hurting from her former fiancé's behavior. Though she hadn't said the exact words, it was clear that she hadn't gotten over his betrayal. The holiday season that once had brought her joy now caused her great pain. Right now, she wasn't in a space to have a relationship with him or any other man.

Not that he was in a place to get involved, either. In a matter of weeks, he was going to be forced out of the army. He was…nowhere with nothing to offer her. Right now he didn't have a present, much less a future, so becoming involved with Hannah was out of the question. Despite knowing that, he couldn't stop thinking about her. Even when they weren't together, his mind was filled with thoughts of her. The way her eyes sparkled when she smiled. The way her wavy hair caressed her shoulders. Her sweet scent that teased and enticed him.

The way her bare skin had glistened after her shower had haunted his thoughts all day. He closed his eyes and forced himself to face the truth. Hannah had consumed his thoughts ever since the first time he'd seen her that summer day. She'd been so beautiful in her yellow floral dress and high-heeled sandals. He'd spotted her walking down Main Street and had been struck still. He didn't know how long he'd stood in the middle of the street before the blare of a car horn had shaken him out of his stupor. Then she'd gotten into a car and driven off, leaving him feeling as if he'd missed out on the greatest opportunity in his life.

He'd been thrilled beyond belief the next evening when he'd spotted her at the cookout Joni and Lex had hosted and hadn't wasted a moment before going up to her and introducing himself.

They'd hit it off as he'd known they would. For the first time in his adult life, he'd believed he could have a lasting relationship with a woman. A real relationship. But that was before he'd gotten injured, back when he'd had something to offer her. Now he was nothing but a broken-down warrior. An old ex-soldier with no future wasn't a catch. He was a burden.

Frowning at the dark turn his thoughts had taken, he stood. After working the stiffness from his leg, he gathered the dirty dishes and the empty wine bottle and went to the kitchen. He rinsed and recycled the bottle, washed the dishes and then went back to the front room. It took only ten minutes to get the furniture back in place. He sat on a chair and stared as the once-roaring fire died down to embers, no longer throwing off heat or giving light.

The fire was the perfect metaphor for his life. Once glorious, now he was useless for anything. Until he had something to offer Hannah, he was going to keep things friendly between them. Strictly platonic. It would be painful as hell, but what choice did he have?

Chapter Nine

"So where are we going?" Hannah asked, trying once more to get an answer.

"What part of it's a surprise don't you understand?" Russell replied, grinning.

He'd been behaving mysteriously ever since he'd picked her up at the boutique an hour ago, right as the last customer had left. Then although she'd told him he didn't have to, he'd pitched in and helped clean and restock the shelves and racks.

"All of it. So tell me."

"Nope."

"Why did I have to change my clothes?" She'd been wearing a yellow jersey dress that showed off every curve she had and silver-and-gold hoop earrings. His eyes had caressed her body, leaving her hot and trembling before he'd told her that she needed to change into something more casual. Pants. Preferably jeans. And comfortable shoes.

"Because, as sexy as you looked—and you did look sexy, by the way—you were overdressed."

"So I take it we aren't going to your brother's restaurant for dinner."

"Will you just get in the car?" he said. "And no, we aren't going to Heaven on Earth. We've done that already."

She settled into the passenger seat of his rental car and fastened her seat belt. He closed her door and then circled the vehicle and climbed in beside her. He winked at her before driving down the street. Clearly he enjoyed keeping her in suspense.

"If I guess will you tell me?"

"No, I won't. If you guess, I'll simply change plans on the fly and never let you know that you were right."

"You will not."

"No. But only because I don't know what else is going on in town."

He turned the car and headed away from downtown Sweet Briar. There was nothing out this way except ranches and the highway.

"You're going the wrong way."

He laughed. "That's funny. You're giving directions when you have absolutely no clue where we're going."

"Maybe not, but I know town is the other way."

"Why, yes, it is. And since we're going in the other direction, you can surmise that we aren't going anywhere in Sweet Briar. I guess that's your first clue."

More than a clue, it was a relief. Lex and Charlotte had gone overboard with the Christmas festivities. In addition to creating new events that admittedly sounded like fun, they must have scoured every newspaper and library book to find any holiday activity that had ever been popular. Of course, Sweet Briar was hosting the usual activities such as a Christkindlmarket on Main Street and Santa's workshop at the youth center. But new activities this year included a madrigal dinner, a Christmas band concert and a production of *A Christmas Carol* at the local high school. Hannah was hoping to avoid those. But now that she and Russell were supposed to be a couple, they might have to show their faces at one or two of these events. If his enthusiasm was anything to go by, he'd be dragging her all over town.

She looked out the window at the passing scenery. The colorful flowers and leaf-filled trees of summer had been replaced by naked branches and brown grass. Although it wasn't as colorful as the warmer months, there was something starkly beautiful about the landscape. It was as if nature had exhausted itself during spring, summer and fall, and was now taking a breather. Being "on" was exhausting, even for Mother Nature.

Hannah certainly found it trying at times. She loved her boutique and adored her friends but smiling and acting as if she didn't have a care in the world took a toll on her. She enjoyed and needed the time she spent alone when she could just be herself. Time when it wasn't necessary for her to be a Positive Polly. Of course, now that Russell was living with her, she didn't have much time alone. But she was discovering that she could be herself and didn't have to put on a happy face for him.

He'd seen the reality of her relationship with her family, such as it was, and he hadn't blinked. Just last night she'd told him the unvarnished truth about her pain, and he'd understood. He hadn't told her that enough time had passed for the hurt to be gone, something she'd often said to herself. As if there was a clock on hurt.

She found his attitude refreshing. Affirming.

After about thirty minutes they arrived in Willow Creek, the nearest big town to Sweet Briar. Willow Creek had the big-box stores and fast-food chains that couldn't be found in Sweet Briar, but it lacked the charm of her hometown.

"So we're going to Walmart?" she joked.

He simply shook his head. "We'll be there in about five minutes. Do you think you can hold out until then?"

She folded her arms over her chest and pretended to pout. "I guess. But I won't be happy about it."

"You really are cute, you know that?"

Her heart pinged once and she forced herself to keep from taking his words to mean something that they didn't. He was just kidding. But why had the joke felt like flirting?

Before she could answer that, he parked the car. She heard the sound of a merry-go-round and turned to look at him. She clapped her hands together in glee. "We're going to the winter carnival?"

"Darn. You guessed. That was my plan. Now I guess I'll have to come up with a plan B." He laughed as he turned the key, starting the ignition.

"Don't you dare. I haven't been to a carnival in forever."

"So I take it you like my plan."

"Absolutely." Willow Creek's winter carnival was well known for being an actual *winter* carnival and not a *Christmas* one so she didn't have to worry about seeing holiday reminders everywhere she went.

They got out of the car and walked down the road. As they drew near, the sounds of laughter and parents calling for their children not to get too far away grew louder and Hannah's heart fluttered with anticipation. Russell reached out and grabbed her hand and tingles skipped down her spine at the contact.

Several middle-school-aged kids darted in their direction and Russell pulled her close to his side, then wrapped his arm around her waist. "We don't want to get separated in the crowd."

She looked around. Although there were a lot of people, the number wasn't so great that there was any risk of losing each other. Not to mention most of the people buzzing around were under five feet tall. "Not possible."

"Humor me."

Since she enjoyed the feel of his body pressed against hers, the warmth that she felt whenever their denim-clad legs brushed as they walked, she didn't argue. She would take her pleasure where she could find it. "What do you want to do first?"

"This is your surprise, so you get to choose."

"The merry-go-round. Unless that will make you dizzy."

He raised an eyebrow at her. "I'm a soldier in the United States Army. I have jumped out of planes, swum in swamps, survived the heat of the deserts and the humidity of jungles."

"So… You're saying you won't get dizzy?" she joked.

"I think I can handle riding on a polka-dot pony."

He purchased tickets and then they stood in line with a bunch of waist-high kids who were talking a mile a minute about what animal they wanted to ride. When the gate opened, the little ones rushed ahead, plowing into Hannah and Russell as they went. By the time Hannah and Russell got on the ride, the polka-dot pony was occupied by a little girl who was pleased that her pants matched her steed, so Russell had to settle for a pink horse.

As the ride started up, Hannah began to think that the merry-go-round was a symbol for her life. She'd been moving ahead and seemed to be making progress. Her boutique was doing well. Her designs were in demand. From the outside, it appeared she had it all together, but in reality, she wasn't going anyplace. At least not emotionally. She was simply going around in circles.

The music ended and the ride slowed to a halt. She and Russell waited until the kids had run off before following. They wandered around, choosing no path in particular but rather randomly ambling in whichever direction struck their fancy, occasionally taking a turn on a ride.

When they came upon the games, Russell smiled and bought a ticket to a target-shooting game. "Pick out the prize you want, and I'll win it for you."

Before she could answer, a little girl leaned

against the counter. She was about six and cute as a button. She glanced at a boy who looked a few years older. "But I want the pink bunny."

"I already told you, Melanie. I don't have any more tickets and no more money," the boy replied.

Tears welled up in the little girl's eyes. "But Tommy, you said you could win it for me."

The boy looked like he wanted to cry himself. "I thought I could. Let's go."

"Wait," Hannah said, pained to see the little girl's disappointment.

"Why?" The boy looked at her suspiciously and then put his arm on the little girl's shoulder protectively, pulling her closer to his side.

"You see that man there? He's my friend. From what he's told me, he's the best shot in the world. He's so good he can shoot with his eyes closed."

"Really?" the little girl asked, inching closer. "Can he win me the pink bunny? My brother tried but he couldn't do it."

"Sure he can. He was just telling me about all the things he can do." Hannah grinned at Russell. "Go ahead. Win the bunny."

Russell picked up the toy shotgun. "I don't know whether to be flattered or not."

"I vote yes."

"Okay then. I'll be flattered." He took aim at the balloons on the back of the stall, pulling the trigger five times in quick succession. Five balloons in a row popped.

The man running the game looked at Russell and then grinned and held out three small trinkets. "Choose."

"What? I shot out all of the balloons. We want the pink bunny."

"That's the megaprize. You need to win five of these smaller prizes in order to win the megaprize."

"Is that right? There's no sign saying that."

The man shrugged. "Those are the rules. Either play or move aside so the next person in line can take a turn."

Hannah frowned. That sounded like false advertising to her.

Russell smiled slowly. "No problem. Line up all the guns." He looked at the little girl. "You'll have your pink bunny in no time. And Hannah, start thinking about which prize you want."

"You're mighty sure of yourself," the man said.

Russell only nodded and picked up the first gun. When he'd emptied all five pellets into five balloons, he picked up the next toy gun and did the same. In under five minutes, he'd shot out every balloon, without missing one.

As he played, a small crowd gathered to watch. By the time he'd finished, he'd won the pink bunny for Melanie, a purple turtle for another child and a yellow elephant for Hannah. He carried the stuffed toy under his arm as they walked away.

"You really are a good shot," Hannah said. She recognized the same awed hero worship in her voice that the little kids had spoken with.

"You sound surprised."

"Maybe a little. You're a soldier so I knew you would be good, but I didn't expect you to be great. You didn't miss a shot."

"Missing a shot can have deadly consequences for me or for someone on my team. So I practice. It's important that I'm able to perform all facets of my job."

There was an odd tone in his voice, but she couldn't name it. It was a mix of confidence and something that sounded like despair. That couldn't be right. Why would he despair? He'd just proved that he was an excellent marksman.

They strolled the grounds until they came upon a skating rink. "Do you skate?" she asked.

"A little. I haven't skated in years."

"It's like riding a bike," she said, pulling him to the booth to rent ice skates. "Actually I'm not sure if that's true or not."

"And you're assuming I know how to ride a bike."

"That's not what it means." She was about to explain what the expression meant when she glanced at his face. He was struggling to hold back laughter.

"I know what the saying means."

She poked him in his side. "So are we skating or not?"

"Yes."

They sat on a bench and swapped their shoes for skates, then stepped up to the rink. Hannah wobbled a moment as she got the feel of the ice. Then pushing off on her left leg, she began gliding across the ice. She did a spin in the middle of the rink, feeling the joy down to her soul. To her ice-skating was better than riding a bike. It was the most fun that she could have by herself.

She made a circuit and then went to where she'd left Russell. He applauded and she took a small bow.

"You've got more skills than you let on," he said. "I'm not sure I can keep up with you. I'll be lucky not to fall."

"Are you telling me the soldier who wrestles alligators in swamps and fights bears in hand-to-hand combat in the woods can't handle a little ice?"

He chuckled. "I don't recall mentioning alligators and bears."

"I read between the lines. Perhaps I shouldn't have embellished."

"Don't get me wrong. I can totally do those things. I just don't like to brag."

"Then let's skate."

"Okay. Surely I can move across the ice without looking like a clown."

With his muscular body, that was the last thing he needed to worry about. He couldn't look like a clown if he was wearing a red nose, an orange wig and face paint.

She offered him her hand and he took it. As always, her skin heated at the contact. Moving slowly, and dodging kids who were skating willy-nilly, they moved around the ice. After circling the rink twice, he gained confidence and the stiffness left his body.

He'd been so impressive when he'd been playing the shooting game. He'd done so well that the man running the game had needed to shut it down temporarily so he could blow up more balloons. Or so he'd said. Hannah suspected that he hadn't wanted Russell to win any more prizes.

Hannah had been so proud to be with him. Although they weren't in a competition, she wanted him to feel the same pride in her. She couldn't shoot like he could, but she was a fairly good skater. This was her time to shine.

She let go of Russell's hand and began to skate backward, performing a basic step sequence while he looked on.

"You're great."

"I love it. I used to skate all the time." Ice skating lessons had been a gift to herself when she'd been in college. She'd watched figure skating on television and had been impressed by the grace the skaters possessed. Being taller than average, she'd felt gawky and awkward growing up. Having a dainty and petite mother and sister only served to make her feel clumsier. When she was on the ice, she found the grace she'd been longing for and hadn't known that she possessed.

She'd stopped skating when her engagement ended and she'd moved to Sweet Briar. True, opening her boutique had taken quite a bit of her time, and there wasn't a rink in town, but if she'd really wanted to skate, she would have found a way. She'd let this simple pleasure slip out of her life without noticing. Now that she was on the ice again, she knew she would find a way to do it more regularly.

She smiled at Russell. He'd given her back a joy she hadn't even known was lost. Gratitude and something that felt suspiciously close to love filled her heart. She let the gratitude stay and kicked the burgeoning feeling to the curb. He didn't want her love so there was no sense in nurturing an emotion that would only lead to disappointment and possibly a broken heart.

Two boys skating wildly came up behind Russell. Before she could warn him, one of the boys crashed into Russell's leg, knocking his feet from under him. He slid across the ice and crashed into the side of the rink. The boys took a tumble as well, but within seconds they were back on their feet.

"Sorry, mister," the smaller one said as the bigger one raced away. "Are you okay?"

Russell nodded and waved at the kid. "Go on."

Hannah skated up to Russell and offered her hand. "Are you really okay?"

Before he could answer, a woman skated over, dragging the bigger kid by the collar of his jacket. "Are you okay? I'm so sorry. I told my sons to be careful."

Russell brushed aside her concern. "No worries. I'm fine."

"He'll be fine," Hannah assured the woman as she slowly skated away, holding tight to her sons. Hannah offered her hand to Russell. "Let me help you up."

He pushed it away. "I don't need help."

He tried to get his skates under him, but unable to get a grip of the ice, his skates slipped and slid.

"You're hurt."

"It's nothing." His voice was gruff. Irritated. "Stop fussing over me like I'm a kid. I'm a—"

"—a man. A soldier in the United States Army." She rolled her eyes. "Did I get that right?"

"You're pretty sassy, you know that?"

"I've been called many things, but never that."

He had to be getting cold sitting on the ice. Or maybe his pride was keeping him warm. She offered him her hand again. When he glared at her, she gave him her best smile. He blew out a breath and then took it. With her help, he was able to stand. They skated back to the entrance and got off the ice. As they walked back to the bench to take off their skates, she noticed that he was favoring his right leg.

They took off their skates and put on their shoes.

"I can return your skates if you need me to," Hannah offered.

He glared at her and stalked back to the skate rental, limping as he went.

"Or not."

She followed him. The earlier pleasure had vanished, popping like one of the balloons in the game Russell had won earlier.

"I guess we should go home," Hannah said. Although there was more to see and do, it wouldn't be fun now that he'd turned into a grouch.

Russell inhaled, his massive chest expanding and straining his leather jacket, before slowly blowing out the breath. "I'm sorry. I shouldn't have taken out my irritation on you."

"I understand. Your leg hurts. You probably shouldn't walk around too much more."

"My leg is fine," he said stiffly. "What do you want to do next?"

"I would love to sit and drink some hot chocolate. And maybe eat a cookie or two."

He looked at her as if trying to determine if she was humoring him. He must have decided she was being honest, because he nodded. "I could go for a warm drink myself."

The concession stand was near the skating rink, so he wouldn't be doing a lot of walking. They grabbed her stuffed elephant and headed over. The line was short and within minutes they'd gotten their orders.

"Let's sit over there," Hannah said, gesturing to tables and chairs near a petting zoo. Excited kids were surrounding goats and pigs, making more noise than the animals. She loved it.

"Okay. But if a goat tries to eat my corn dog, I might have to take him out."

"I don't think they can get over here," Hannah said. Nevertheless, she took a seat at a table closer to the middle. Instead of a cookie, she'd gotten a hot dog and a funnel cake to go with her hot chocolate. It wasn't the most nutritious meal, nor was it dinner at Heaven on Earth, but sitting here with Russell, none of that mattered. She was having the time of her life.

That brief moment when he'd turned grumpy had passed and he was once more charming. As they ate, they talked about everything and nothing.

"Do you mind if I ask you a question?" she said when there was a lull in the conversation. "If it's none of my business, tell me and I'll shut up."

He paused, his corn dog halfway to his mouth, then nodded cautiously. "Okay."

"What's up with your leg?"

"You saw. That kid crashed into me."

"I did. But I noticed before that you were limping. And it seems to bother you at the shop on occasion. So, what gives?"

He frowned and she thought he wouldn't answer. Maybe he was about to turn into a Grinch again. She didn't want their good time to end, but she cared about him. He was showing himself to be a good friend and she wanted to be the same. "I got hurt on a mission."

"Where? What happened?"

"The where is classified as are the details of the mission."

"Of course. I understand that. But can you tell me about your knee? What is the injury? How long will it take you to get back to one hundred percent?"

"Depends on what you mean by one hundred percent. Will I be able to live and function like any other man on this leg? Absolutely. Therapy can work wonders. From day to day I'm getting better. I no longer have to take pain pills just to walk. And as you've seen, I can walk and even run." He winced. "I'm just not so good on ice skates."

That sounded good. So why did he sound so bleak? And what wasn't he saying? "But what about returning to your job in the army? Is that in question?"

He shook his head slowly and she knew then what he hadn't said.

"Not any longer. According to the doctors, my leg has improved as much as it's going to. Unfortunately for me, it hasn't improved enough for me to continue to be a soldier. The military is currently in the process of giving me a medical discharge. I have twenty years of service so I'm retiring."

"Wow."

"Yeah. Wow."

She didn't know anything about army requirements, or how close he could have been to meeting them. But she did know about people. And pain of disappointment. And Russell was obviously in pain. It was clear that he was trying to disguise it. And she knew her pity was the last thing he wanted.

"You've been in the army a long time."

"Since I was eighteen."

"Wow. Did you always want to be a soldier?"

"Not always."

"Why did you decide to join?"

"When I was in high school, I got my girlfriend pregnant."

"Oh. I didn't know you had a child."

He crumpled his empty paper plate in his fist. "I don't."

"I see."

"I doubt it." He chuckled, but there was no mirth in the sound. Then he sighed. "When Tricia told me she was pregnant, I was shocked, which was especially stupid all things considered. I knew where babies came from. I'd been planning to go to college in the fall, but I knew I couldn't. I'd been raised to know that a man didn't run from his responsibilities, and I was about to have a child to support. I wanted to be a full-time father, not just a dad on the weekends, so I asked her to marry me. Then I joined the army."

He swallowed the last of his drink, then crushed the paper cup and set it beside the ruined plate. "Anyway, she told me she didn't want to get married. I tried to talk her into it, but she told me she wanted to go to college. Tricia was the smartest kid in our class by far. She'd gotten perfect scores on the SAT and the ACT. I never could figure out why a brilliant girl like her would be interested in a jock like me. Apparently she wasn't. Not really. She said she could be a single mother and go to college. Her parents were going to help her with the baby. Other people who weren't nearly as smart as Tricia had done it so I knew it was possible. Even though we weren't going to get married, I still had a child on the way. Until I didn't. A few weeks after she'd dropped that bomb on me, she told me she'd lost the baby."

"I'm so sorry to hear that. You must have been devastated."

"We both were. People kept saying it was for the best because we were so young and had the rest of our lives to have kids, which didn't help matters." He shook his head. "As if we were supposed to be glad our baby had died."

"People can be idiots even when they mean well."

"You'll get no argument here."

"So why did you still join the army instead of going to college?"

"Because talking to the recruiter made me realize that I actually wanted to be a soldier. That was what I'd been born to do. Being a soldier is more than my job. It's my calling. It's who I am. Does that make sense to you?"

She nodded. She knew that many people had callings even though she didn't personally feel like she had one. Sure, she liked designing clothes and owning her own business, but it didn't reach the level of a calling. It wasn't as noble as what Russell had done and obviously wanted to continue to do. Sadly, he couldn't. "Whatever happened with Tricia?"

"She went to Wellesley College and excelled. I've missed my class reunions, but from what I hear she's done very well for herself."

"You sound happy for her. Proud, even."

"Why shouldn't I be? I don't hate her. I never

did. I was disappointed that she didn't want to marry me, but I got over it."

"Were you heartbroken?"

"I was eighteen."

She remembered being devastated when her high school boyfriend broke up with her a month before prom. Back then she couldn't imagine life without him. Now she wouldn't be able to pick him out of a one-man lineup.

"At the time I thought I was in love with her," Russell continued. "But who knows? Maybe I was just horny. The point is, like most high school sweethearts, we didn't make it as a couple. Does that mean I should wish her a lifetime of misery? No. I've been happy with my life and it's good to know she's been the same."

"You're a good man, Russell Danielson."

"I do my best."

They sat there in silence for a few more minutes, as if her heartfelt words had given them each something to ponder. Then they rose together and took their trash to the garbage can. His leg seemed to be bothering him more than before, but she didn't see the point in mentioning it. It was his leg and he knew how it felt.

"I've had a good time, but I'm getting a bit cold. Ready to call it a night?" she said instead.

"You don't want to ride on the Ferris wheel?"

She shook her head. "No. I don't like them.

They make me dizzy and sitting at the top and looking down does weird things to my stomach."

"Really? I thought you were fearless."

"That would be you. You're fearless and I'm sassy."

He grabbed her hand and they walked back to the car. She took small, slow steps, determined to keep him from putting additional strain on his leg.

The ride home was pleasant and passed much too quickly for her satisfaction. When they stepped inside her house, she kissed his cheek. His normally clean-shaven jaw was now covered with stubble that tickled her lips, making them tingle. "Thanks. I can't think of the last time I had this much fun. It was a wonderful surprise."

"The pleasure was all mine."

She said good-night, then grabbed her stuffed elephant and headed to her room. This night had been among the best of her life and she hadn't wanted it to end. But kissing Russell's cheek had made her long for more kisses and she didn't want to mar the evening with another rejection. She'd have to be content with the friendship he'd offered and not long for a different type of relationship.

Too bad that was easier said than done.

Chapter Ten

Russell grabbed the rail and looked up the flight of stairs. With the way his knee felt, the thirteen steps may as well have been a hundred. His leg was killing him. It had been throbbing ever since the kid had slammed into him on the ice. His knee had been on the mend but without a doubt he'd suffered a setback. He wouldn't know how much damage had been done until morning. In the meantime, he would soak in the tub. Hopefully that would do some good.

If he'd had a lick of sense, he would have left the carnival the minute Hannah had suggested it. They'd already been there a couple of hours and had had lots of fun. But he hadn't wanted the evening to end. Watching Hannah enjoy herself had filled him with pleasure. If he hadn't gotten injured, she would have continued skating. The underlying sorrow that had been hovering around her had vanished. He'd wanted her to have more time to be carefree and have fun.

But that wasn't the only reason he hadn't wanted to leave. His pride had been a major factor. He'd seen the admiration in her eyes when he'd won the stuffed pink rabbit for that little girl. Melanie had grinned and clapped when he'd handed her the prize. Her brother had thanked him profusely. Their appreciation had felt good. But it was the look in Hannah's eyes that had made him feel like a hero. No. More than that. He'd felt like a whole man.

A man who'd do anything to hold on to the respect and admiration of his woman.

He could have stopped once he'd won Melanie's pink bunny but he'd enjoyed showing off for Hannah. Although the crowd had applauded his every victory, he'd been performing for an audience of one.

Thank goodness she couldn't see him now. There was nothing heroic about being unable to stand because he'd been foolish. He'd waited in the living room until he was sure she was asleep. Now he could limp up the stairs without risk of lowering her opinion of him. The last thing he wanted was for her to see him in a weak moment. Unable to do something as basic as walking up a flight of stairs. Hell, before the accident he would have been able to run up these stairs carrying a hundred-pound pack on his back without breaking a sweat. Now he was panting and he hadn't reached the middle yet.

A part of him knew that he was being ridiculous. Accidents happened all the time. This was more than being unable to climb a flight of stairs. It was facing his changing reality. He'd always known he wouldn't be able to be a soldier forever. But he'd believed he'd had more time than this. He was only thirty-eight years old. He was still in his prime.

Exhaling, he pulled himself up the last stairs and limped to the bathroom. While the tub filled with warm water, he undressed, being extra careful as he dragged the jeans over his swollen knee. He sank into the water and closed his eyes.

Leaning back, he let the images of the day flash in front of his eyes. He pictured Hannah as she'd tried to cajole him into telling her what he'd planned for their date. She'd been so cute, so charming, that he'd almost given in. But that would have meant ruining the surprise. And he would have missed the delighted expression on her face when she'd realized they were at the winter carnival.

He'd never been one for carnivals—he didn't find the games especially challenging and he wasn't a fan of the rides—but he'd thought going would make Hannah happy. And he'd been right. She'd enjoyed herself immensely. There was nothing to remind Hannah of the broken heart that she'd endured three Christmases ago.

Hopefully little by little she would be able to put the past behind her. With his help, she'd realize that Christmas and her broken engagement were two separate things. Then she'd be able to enjoy the season once more as she deserved.

The water cooled and he climbed out of the tub. His knee wasn't aching as badly as it had been earlier, giving him some hope that the damage had been minimal. He dried off, wrapped the towel around his waist and walked slowly to his room. The part of his brain that didn't know what was good for him had hoped he'd run into Hannah in the hallway.

No such luck tonight. He pulled on a pair of gym shorts and climbed into bed, shifting as he tried unsuccessfully to get comfortable. He'd finally decided to put a pillow beneath his leg when there was a knock on the door.

Before he could answer, Hannah stuck her head inside. "Hey. I know you're awake. How's your leg?"

"It's fine."

The room was suddenly bright as she turned on the overhead light and he blinked as his eyes adjusted.

"Really? Then why do you have it propped on a pillow?"

"Did it occur to you that I might like sleeping this way?"

"Not once. Did it occur to you that you don't have to be macho man around me? That it's okay to be human. You're hurt. Let me help."

Not waiting for a reply, she crossed the small room and stood beside his bed. She was dressed in a blue nightgown that covered her from chin to ankles. It wasn't revealing at all, but she still looked sexy and his imagination went into overdrive.

She looked down at him. The sweet expression on her face was nearly his undoing. How could she be at once innocent and beguiling? "Is it okay if I sit down beside you?"

He didn't trust himself to speak, didn't know if he had the voice anyway, so he nodded and scooted over, making room for her. Without saying a word, she gracefully lowered herself to the bed. Her sweet scent immediately surrounded him and his imagination traveled to places it had no business going. Her thick wavy hair fell around her shoulders as she bent to inspect his knee, obscuring her face momentarily. When her soft hand touched his skin, heat surged through his body and he sucked in a breath. This had to be the most delicious torture known to man.

Her hand moved gently over his knee as she inspected it. The feel of her fingers aroused him, and he gasped. She jerked her hand back immediately. "Sorry. I didn't mean to hurt you."

"You didn't." His voice was raspy. Needing to hide his growing desire for her, he spoke harshly. "But you're not helping, either."

If she was offended, she covered it well. "Maybe you should go to the doctor."

"I'm not interested in driving to Charlotte or wherever it is you people in small towns go when you get sick."

She smirked, looking cuter than she should have. His attempt to erect a wall between them was going up in flames. "We *people* see Rick Tyler, our town doctor. Tomorrow is Sunday and he doesn't have office hours, but he opens for emergencies. If you want, I'll call him in the morning and ask him if we can stop by his office."

"Why do you care so much about my knee? This whole thing…" He waved his hands between them. "It's only make-believe. We're only pretending to be in love."

This relationship—or whatever it was between them—would end. It had to. They'd agreed to that on day one. When he'd proposed the arrangement, he'd done it to help Hannah and later himself. He'd never intended for feelings to grow between them. Not this deep or this real. And certainly not this quickly. He wasn't sure which way to turn.

In the past, he'd been able to recognize women who'd wanted a commitment and had studiously avoided them. With his career, he hadn't stayed in one place for long. There hadn't been time to become deeply involved, much less put down roots or start a family. He'd known it would be unfair to start something he'd be unable or unwilling to finish. He'd never complained about the instability that was part and parcel of army life. He'd known what he was getting into when he'd signed on the dotted line.

But this thing with Hannah had sprung out of nowhere and it was spiraling out of control. His feelings for her were getting jumbled and he was having a hard time separating real from make-believe. He needed to draw a bright red line between the two. If he had to force himself to be gruff in order to accomplish that goal, and possibly anger Hannah in the process, then so be it. It would be better in the long run.

"I know that. But we don't have to be in love for me to care about you. We're friends and I want to help. The same way you wanted to help me with my family when you kissed me. You weren't in love with me. In fact, we'd barely been friends.

But we've gotten to know each other better and we've grown so much closer since then. Don't you think?"

He nodded because she seemed to expect a response, but he was only partially agreeing with what she'd said. It was true that he'd wanted to help her with her family. But that wasn't the only reason he'd kissed her. He'd kissed her because he'd wanted to. She'd been on his mind ever since that day they'd spent together. Whenever he'd closed his eyes, he pictured her as she'd been that summer day. She'd been so gorgeous, her brown skin glowing in the sunlight. Back then he'd resisted the urge to kiss her. He'd had to leave the next day and had wanted to take it slowly.

But when he'd seen her in the boutique a few days ago, he'd jumped at the first excuse to take her into his arms. And her family had given him one. Once their lips had met, he'd lost control of himself and he'd been swept away with passion. He'd even forgotten there were other people present until they'd been rudely interrupted.

If things were different, he'd suggest that they convert this pretend relationship into a real one. But things weren't different. He was gradually coming to accept that the doctors were right. He would improve and be able to live a normal life— hell, he was doing that now. But he'd never be healthy enough to be a soldier again. He had to figure out his next step.

He had no idea how long that would take or where he would land. But he knew one thing. He couldn't drag Hannah along for the bumpy ride when he didn't know how—or where—it would end.

"So as your friend," she continued, "I'm offering to call the doctor for you."

He could keep being stubborn, but there was no point. Hannah wasn't going to relent. "Let's see what tomorrow brings."

"Okay."

She just sat there. He was enjoying her presence but being alone with her was too tempting. "Anything else?"

"There's a movie coming on in a few minutes that I want to watch."

He nodded, certain that more was forthcoming.

"Do horror movies scare you?"

"You're kidding, right?"

"Of course. For a moment there I forgot who I was talking to. Nothing frightens you. Especially on a TV screen. But that's not true for me. I scare easily and scary movies make it hard to sleep. So if you aren't too tired, do you mind watching it with me?"

"Let me get this straight," he said. "You want

to watch a movie even though it'll probably give you nightmares?"

She nodded. "It's really popular. Everybody else has already seen it. They make references to it and I'm lost because I don't know what they're talking about. But if you watch it with me, I know I won't be scared."

"Fine." With the way his knee was hurting, he wasn't going to be able to sleep anyway. He may as well be distracted by a movie. Throwing off his blanket, he started to stand.

"What are you doing?"

"Getting up so I can go downstairs."

"That's not necessary. You have a TV in here. Besides, you need to stay off your leg."

Before he could argue, Hannah had grabbed the remote from the side table and was scooting across the bed. In a blink, she was under the blanket. Sighing, he covered himself again. He leaned his pillow against the headboard and sat up. Every inch of his willpower was about to be tested, but what could he do? This was Hannah's house. Her bedroom, even though he was temporarily calling it his own. He certainly couldn't kick her out.

Hannah smiled at him and his internal debate ended. He'd lost. He couldn't think of a good reason why he and Hannah couldn't watch this movie in his room together. And he truly didn't want her to leave. When the title came on, he realized it was a movie he'd seen before. He hadn't found it to be especially frightening, but it had been enjoyable.

As the movie played, he found himself watching Hannah more than the television. She was positively enchanting. And truly frightened. For the life of him, he didn't understand why she would deliberately scare herself silly. There were plenty of other options available. At this time of year, she could watch any number of heartwarming movies designed to make her smile. But then, she didn't want reminders of the season.

He frowned as he thought of just how much Hannah's family and her former fiancé had stolen from her. They'd not only taken her trust. They'd robbed her of the ability to enjoy the Christmas season. He couldn't give her forever. But he could restore her love of Christmas.

Hannah squealed and jumped, grabbing his arm and snapping him out of his thoughts. Laughing, he pulled her close to him. In an instant all of his mirth vanished and he was filled with desire. But it was a desire he wouldn't act on. Hannah was his friend. She deserved a commitment—something he couldn't give her. So he forced his lust aside. "Are you sure you want to watch this?"

She nodded, her head buried in his shoulder. Her enticing scent intoxicated him, making it hard to think of anything but her. "Just tell me when this scene is over."

He nodded and forced himself to concentrate on the movie. She scooted closer. This was the most fun he'd had in bed in months. "It's done."

"Thanks." Hannah pulled her head back and grinned at him.

"No worries."

They watched the movie without talking much. Or he watched the movie. Hannah either covered her eyes with her hands or hid her face against his chest for over half of it.

When the credits rolled, Hannah leaned against the headboard. "That was really good."

He chuckled. "How would you know? I never expected you to be such a chicken."

"Chicken?" She poked him in the shoulder. "You're going to be sorry for that, pal."

He didn't know what she meant so he was totally caught off guard when she tickled him.

He barked out a laugh and twisted away. "Two can play that game." He started tickling her in return. She squirmed against him and immediately his body became engulfed in flames. Their eyes met and held. Slowly he lowered his head and kissed her. She tasted so good. So sweet. Because she was. She deserved all the best in the world. But he had nothing to offer her.

He pulled back, then leaned his forehead against hers. "Sorry. I got carried away for a moment. I think you should leave."

She closed her eyes briefly and he wondered what she was thinking. If she gave the slightest indication that she wanted to stay his willpower would go up in smoke. She nodded and silently climbed out of his bed and left.

"You did the right thing," he muttered to himself when she was gone.

So why did letting her leave feel like the biggest mistake he'd ever made?

Hannah stared at her bedroom door. She was fully dressed and had been for twenty minutes. Yet she couldn't find the nerve to open the door. Whenever she thought about leaving this sanctuary, she recalled what happened last night and embarrassment assaulted her, making her stomach churn.

Everything had started innocently enough. They'd had a great time at the carnival up until he'd been hurt. His leg had obviously been bothering him after he'd been knocked onto the ice, but stubborn man that he was, he'd continued to walk on it. By the time they'd gotten home it was clear that he'd needed to soak his knee, so she'd headed up to bed so he could use the tub.

But she couldn't stop worrying about him. She'd planned to make a quick check to assure herself that he was all right and then return to her room. But they'd had a nice conversation and she'd lingered longer than she'd intended. Things felt comfortable between them so watching the movie while sharing a bed had seemed harmless. And it had been until she'd touched him. Then desire had gripped her and she'd had to struggle to maintain her cool. Over and over she'd reminded herself that he wasn't interested in her and that they had no future. Somehow she'd managed to regain control and keep her feelings hidden while they'd watched the film.

All she'd had to do was say good-night and leave the room once the credits had rolled. If she'd stuck to that plan, she wouldn't have humiliated herself. And this morning she'd be able to cook breakfast for him.

Instead she'd pounced on him like a love-starved old maid. Well, she couldn't hide in here forever. It was time to face the music. Squaring her shoulders, she crossed the room, opened the door and went downstairs to the kitchen. Ever since Russell had come to stay with her, he'd prepared breakfast for her before she went to work. Since she didn't open her shop until noon on Sundays, she could cook breakfast for him. Besides, she didn't know how his knee was holding up and if she'd need to contact Dr. Tyler.

She gathered the ingredients she needed to make waffles and set them on the table. She grabbed the waffle iron, turned and nearly bumped into

Russell. Startled, she lost her hold on the waffle iron and it began to slide from her hands. Russell reached out, caught it and then placed it on the table.

"How's the knee?" she asked. She focused on his denim-clad legs instead of looking into his eyes.

He raised his leg and then bent and straightened his knee several times before setting his foot back on the floor. "Good as new. I just needed to rest it."

"That's good to hear."

"What are you making?"

"Besides waffles? I thought I'd make bacon and scramble some eggs."

"Want help?"

"You've cooked for me since you've gotten here. It's only fair that I return the favor."

"Sounds good to me."

He pulled out a chair and sat quietly at the table. So much for her having time alone to lick her wounds. But then, this might be better. Sort of like ripping off a Band-Aid. She'd never liked pulling off her bandages. She'd preferred to soak them in water until the glue loosened and they just floated off.

Telling herself to concentrate, she mixed the batter and then poured it into the hot waffle iron. Puttering around in the kitchen and trying out new recipes was one of her secret pleasures although she didn't do it often. Cooking for one wasn't as much fun as cooking for someone else and sharing the meal.

At first she was self-conscious cooking in front of Russell, but with every passing second she felt more at ease. By the time she set their plates on the table and he'd poured coffee for each of them. The embarrassment from the previous night had faded.

"What time do you close the store on Sundays?"

"Five." Stores in big cities might have longer hours, but she needed time to recharge and work on her designs. She might be missing out on sales by being open for only half a day, but that was a trade-off she was willing to make.

"Good. That gives us some time."

"Time for what?"

He grimaced. "Joni texted me earlier. It seems my parents came to town a couple of days early to spend time with the grandkids. And since I only asked her not to tell them I was here to keep them from rushing down, she didn't see a reason to keep it a secret and spilled the beans." He took another sip of his coffee.

"Okay. But why do I get the feeling there's more to the story than what you're telling me?"

"You're not just another gorgeous face, are you? Joni being Joni, she told them about you. They can't wait to meet my new girlfriend. We're invited to Brandon's for dinner tonight."

"Oh." Her heart began to pound and her stomach churned.

"Yes. It's time for you to meet the parents."

Chapter Eleven

Hannah inhaled deeply and reached for Russell's hand. The time had come. She couldn't believe she was actually nervous about meeting Russell's parents. It didn't make sense. It wasn't as if she was really his girlfriend and wanted their acceptance. Once the pretend relationship ended, Hannah doubted she'd see them again. Besides, she'd met them before, if briefly. Mrs. Danielson had complimented her on the wedding dress she'd designed for Arden. But that had been a couple of years ago. Hannah doubted that the inconsequential interaction at her son's wedding had made a big impact on Mrs. Danielson. She might not even remember the encounter.

"You can't possibly be nervous," Russell said.

"I can't? And yet I am."

"Why?"

"You can't possibly be that dense," she said, deliberately using his words.

He blinked and then laughed. They'd reached Brandon's front stairs, but instead of climbing them, he stepped in front of her. "What's going on inside that beautiful head of yours?"

Her heart skipped a beat at his words and the affection in his voice. She warned herself to be on guard so she wouldn't confuse fact and fiction. She'd been doing a good job before. Now her imagination was running wild. The funny thing was, until the two of them had entered into this fake relationship, her thoughts about Russell had been limited.

In the short time that they'd been pretending to be in love, she'd begun imagining what could happen between them. If only he wanted her as more than a friend. If only he didn't need to return to his army base after the holidays to complete the paperwork so he could retire. *If only...* The two saddest words in the world.

"I know this relationship between us isn't real, but your family doesn't. That means your parents are going to be trying to get to know me. Studying me. Questioning me. Determining if I'm good enough for their firstborn son."

"That's not at all what's going to happen. If anything they're going to be trying to figure out why a sweet, wonderful, gorgeous woman like you is interested in a broken-down soldier like me."

"You're not broken down. Far from it." Though she tried, she couldn't keep her eyes from sweeping over his body. Rather than wearing his customary jeans, he'd dressed in black slacks and a gray pullover that accentuated the breadth of his chest and the strength in his shoulders. Forcing her eyes back to his, she was startled by the flame of heat flickering there. But then he blinked and the fire was extinguished, and once more his eyes were clear and friendly. She wasn't deceived by his demeanor. She'd seen the smoldering desire.

He smiled but she saw a hint of sadness there. This wasn't the first time that he'd referred to himself as broken down. She wondered if that was how he saw himself. His description certainly didn't come anywhere near how she saw him, and she believed her opinion was closer to the truth than his.

"Come on. Let's get going." They climbed the stairs and rang the doorbell. "In case I didn't mention it earlier, you look great tonight."

Her heart fluttered. "Thanks."

She'd taken extra care with her appearance.

When she'd gotten home from the boutique, she'd taken a soothing bath and then put on one of her latest creations. Although she had most of her garments mass-produced to sell in her boutique, every once in a while, she made something exclusively for herself. The fitted emerald green dress with the removable cape was one such design. She'd found a clutch in the exact shade and had pumps dyed to match.

He brushed his knuckles under her chin and lifted her face for a soft kiss. She knew he'd been trying to reassure her, but when his lips touched hers, he ignited a fire inside her. It took all of her self-discipline to keep from wrapping her arms around his neck and showing him just how turned on she was.

"It seems like I'm always catching you guys in a clinch."

Hannah heard her friend's voice and turned as Joni and Lex walked up the stairs, each of them holding one of their son's hands as he toddled between them. Joshua's legs weren't quite long enough for him to climb, so they lifted him and set him on each step, much to his delight. Hannah pretended to be interested in the boy's efforts, using the time to gather herself.

"Yeah. Your timing is really bad," Russell said.

The door swung open to reveal Brandon standing there. "Just in time. Come on in."

Russell gave Hannah's hand an encouraging squeeze as she stepped inside. There were hugs and kisses as the elder Danielsons greeted their children. Once they'd all said their hellos, they turned their eyes to Hannah, who was suddenly the center of attention, a situation she'd always tried to avoid.

"Do you remember Hannah?" Russell asked. "You met her at Brandon and Arden's wedding."

"Of course," Mr. Danielson said. He was as tall as his sons and was an older version of Russell with slight differences. While Russell had chosen to shave his head, his father had close-cropped salt-and-pepper hair. But he had the same friendly smile as his son and Hannah felt instantly at ease. "Hello."

"It's a pleasure to see you again, sir."

"What's with this *sir*? Please call me Ross."

"And you can call me Valerie," Russell's mother said. Her smile was just as warm as her husband's and Hannah knew the evening would be as pleasant as Russell had promised.

"Okay. It's nice seeing you again."

Valerie smiled. "You, too. Is that dress another of your designs?"

Hannah nodded.

"It's gorgeous. I'd love to see your other clothes. Perhaps I'll stop by your boutique while I'm in town. That is, if you carry clothes for the older, less trim set. I have a bit too much hip to wear a dress like that."

"Who are you calling older? You're still a young chick," Ross said, giving his wife a squeeze. Valerie grinned and kissed his cheek. "And your hips are perfect, just like the rest of you."

Hannah smiled at the affectionate couple. There was something so sweet about the open way they interacted with each other.

No wonder Russell was so comfortable with displays of affection. He'd been raised by demonstrative parents. Of course, Russell's kisses and embraces were part of the act and intended to keep his family from becoming suspicious, so they didn't count. He wasn't in love with her.

Hannah wondered how he usually interacted with the women he brought home to meet his family. Was he as openly affectionate with them? Did he kiss them? Embrace them? Hold their hands?

Something that felt an awful lot like jealousy consumed Hannah as she imagined Russell with a woman he actually loved. A woman he wanted to share his future with. She forced that negative emotion away. What did it matter? He saw her as a friend and nothing more. Pretending to be in love wouldn't change how he felt. Too bad it wasn't like that for her. Her feelings for him were becoming more real each day.

"Are you okay?" Russell whispered. He leaned

close and his warm breath stirred her hair and goose bumps popped up on her arms.

She turned and their eyes met. For a moment everyone else in the room vanished and it was only the two of them. "I'm fine. I'm actually a little bit relieved. Your parents are great."

"Of course they are. Otherwise I wouldn't be the wonderful man that you know and love."

Laughing, she gave him a gentle poke in the side. She knew he was only kidding but truthfully, he was a wonderful man. The best she'd ever met. The more time she spent with him, the more they interacted, the more wonderful he became. But she wouldn't fool herself. He was only playing the role of a smitten boyfriend.

He'd fooled her family. Now it was time to return the favor by playing the part of the devoted girlfriend. She was going to be the best, most affectionate girlfriend anyone had ever had. With her growing feelings, it wouldn't take much acting.

Brandon excused himself to check on dinner. A few minutes later he announced that everything was ready. Russell took her hand as they went to the dining room. The table was set with exquisite china, crystal and silver.

"You've outdone yourself," Valerie said.

"It's not every day I have my parents and siblings for dinner. With you guys living in Chicago and Russell living God knows where, I had to make it special."

Valerie kissed Brandon's cheek before sitting in the chair her husband held for her.

As Hannah took her seat, she couldn't help wishing she'd been raised in such a loving family. Her father had died when she was a child and she remembered very little about him. Eleanor had been so busy trying to find her next meal ticket that she'd erased all reminders of him from their home. After she'd remarried, they'd moved away to a bigger house in a better neighborhood, a pattern that had repeated throughout Hannah's childhood.

But Hannah couldn't remember a single one of Eleanor's husbands looking at her with the adoration and affection that Ross showed Valerie. In addition to being in love with her, it was clear that he genuinely liked her. They weren't just an old married couple who were still madly in love. What they shared was something much rarer and much more valuable. They were old friends.

That was something Hannah could never say about Eleanor and her revolving cast of spouses. But then, Hannah didn't think her mother actually cared about being liked. Maybe it hadn't mattered to her whether or not she'd been loved. She'd wanted only the money and status that her husbands could provide.

When Hannah had been about twelve, her mother had married Arthur Halloran. He'd been the one stepfather whom Hannah had loved. Arthur had taken a genuine interest in her. He'd listened while she'd droned on for hours about fabric and fashion. He'd admired the sketches for dresses that she'd drawn on loose-leaf paper. One Christmas he'd bought her a sewing machine and a variety of fabrics. He'd proudly worn the shirt with the slightly crooked buttons that she'd sewn for him. But like all her mother's "special friends" and the stepfather who came after him, he hadn't been in her life for long. Once the divorce had been finalized, Eleanor hadn't allowed him to keep in touch with Hannah. The only good father figure she'd had had been torn from her life after three short years.

Watching Russell's family interact, the laughter and warmth they shared, she wondered what it must have felt like to be raised with such love. The security that came from growing up knowing he was wanted. Valued. She couldn't change her family, but for the time being, she would be included in this one.

As she cut into her tender roast, she listened as the older couple answered Russell's questions about former neighbors and friends, then talked about their drive from Chicago to Sweet Briar.

The conversation switched to Russell and questions about his recent exploits in the army. Hannah listened to his answers with particular interest. Though she and Russell were getting to know each other, she didn't feel comfortable interrogating him. Luckily his family had no such reservations.

He gave her a rueful smile before answering his parents' questions. Hannah soon recognized the theme. Was he eating enough? What kind of food? Hopefully not processed MREs. Was he getting enough rest? Did he need them to send him anything? They didn't ask about missions or places he'd been. They were only concerned about Russell's well-being. Hannah noticed that he didn't bring up his injury or his status with the army. She didn't have time to dwell on it because his parents soon changed the subject. *To her*.

"So, tell us more about designing for the stars," Valerie said. "I read in one of those celebrity magazines that you've been hired to design for everyone who's anyone." She listed several very famous people. In her wildest dreams Hannah might be asked to create clothes for them. In reality, it hadn't happened.

Hannah laughed. "I read that, too."

Valerie sighed, clearly disappointed. "So are you telling me that's not true?"

"Not all of it. I have been approached by two of the people you mentioned who want me to design special dresses, but there's nothing concrete yet. It might not amount to anything. Right now I'm designing clothes for the line that I sell at my boutique."

"You should see Hannah's shop, Mom," Russell said. "It's really something. The moment you step inside you'll think you're shopping on the Gold Coast."

"What's the Gold Coast?" Hannah asked.

"It's an exclusive shopping district in Chicago," Valerie explained before turning back to Russell. "But I want to know how you know so much about Hannah's boutique."

"Because I've been there," Russell replied easily before eating some of Brandon's delicious macaroni and cheese.

"He actually helped me for a few days when my saleswomen couldn't work. I was alone and I don't know what I would have done without him."

"What on earth could he do? Surely he wasn't recommending clothes."

"Believe it or not, his opinion was in high demand. It turns out that my customers liked having a man's opinion. Of course, those same women paid no attention to what their husbands thought, so maybe it was just Russell's point of view they wanted. A woman likes looking good for a handsome man."

Russell actually blushed. Lex, Brandon and Ross razzed him for a few minutes.

"Actually," Hannah said, once the kidding had ended, "Russell used those big muscles of his to carry boxes for me. And believe me, I appreciated having him there."

Russell picked up her hand and brushed a kiss against it. "Glad to help."

The women sighed. Hannah had a feeling she might have sighed, too, if she'd been a witness instead of a co-conspirator. One thing was undeniable. Russell was a great actor, convincing everyone of his devotion. Heck, she knew he was only pretending, yet she was getting swept away in the moment.

The conversation shifted to more general topics and Hannah released a pent-up breath. She liked Russell's parents. They were friendly and easy to talk to. Even so, she'd been concerned that she would slip up and give away the game. Or worse yet, say the wrong thing and make them wonder what Russell could possibly see in her. Happily, they'd seemed to like her and were proud of all that she'd accomplished.

They finished dessert and then went into the family room. Brandon stood in the center of the room with his arms outstretched. Russell shook his head. "I know you aren't challenging me."

"To what?" Hannah asked. Clearly she'd missed something.

"Anything," Joni answered. "When we were

growing up, Russell could beat us at any game and did so regularly and without mercy." She waved her hand around, taking in the pile of board games on the table. The chess and checkerboards were ready to go. Hannah noticed there was a pool table near the windows.

"Pick your poison," Brandon said.

"You know it's pool," Russell said, pushing up the sleeves on his sweater. "But I have to warn you that I'm even better than I was before. I've been on some pretty remote bases where the only entertainment was pool."

Brandon grinned. "I have a table in my house. That should tell you something."

The two brothers faced off and then grabbed cues. Hannah and the rest of the family sat down, making friendly wagers on which brother would emerge victorious.

"I can't believe you missed that shot," Brandon said. "If I didn't know better I'd swear you were letting me win."

If only that was the case. The truth was Russell had missed some shots that any other day he could make blindfolded. But on any other day, Hannah wasn't watching his every move, living and dying with each shot. He wanted to impress her so badly that he was making silly mistakes.

"I'm just letting you get overconfident before I move in for the kill."

"Right."

Russell ignored the sarcasm in his brother's voice and the smirk on his face. "I've got you just where I want you."

"About to win?"

Russell moved away from the table, letting Brandon study the remaining balls. Though it would have been wiser to stand where he couldn't see Hannah, Russell clearly wasn't the brightest bulb on the tree. He went and stood beside her chair. So not only could he see her gorgeous legs, which she'd crossed at the ankles, he could also feel the warmth emanating from her body. Every time he inhaled, he got a whiff of her tantalizing scent. No wonder he couldn't focus on the game.

Brandon made one shot and then missed the other.

Arden groaned and slapped a hand across her forehead. "You're letting him back in the game. Next time, go in for the kill."

Russell laughed. His normally sweet and charming sister-in-law was a take-no-prisoners type. Who knew?

"You can do it," Hannah said, cheering him on.

As Russell took his aim, he glanced over at her, which was probably a mistake. She smiled and blew him a kiss just as he was shooting. His stick glanced off the cue ball, which barely moved.

Brandon hooted, then came and stood beside him. As he bent over to pick up the chalk, he whispered in Russell's ear. "I'm beginning to see what the problem is."

"What's that?"

"You're showing off for your girl."

Russell didn't bother to deny it. Although Russell's career and the miles it placed between him and his family meant he didn't see them as much as he'd like, his brother knew him as well as anyone.

Now that he was around his family, he wondered why he'd planned on avoiding them in the first place. After everyone on base had made a point of sticking their noses in his business, he'd convinced himself that his family would do the same. He should have known better. Although his siblings and parents could be opinionated at times, they would never barge in where they weren't wanted. He could tell his family what was going on with him. But not now. After Christmas.

Brandon made his next two shots, winning the game.

Russell clapped his brother on the shoulder. "Good game."

"I would have let you win, but I needed to show off for my own woman."

"I understand. We'll have to play again without an audience."

"Sounds like a plan."

Hannah approached the brothers and put her arm around Russell's waist, then leaned her head on his shoulder. "Oh, well. Maybe next time."

When she was this close, he felt like a winner. "Maybe so."

They played a few board games before the evening came to an end. He was just as entranced by Hannah as he'd been while shooting pool, so he'd lost those games, too. Not that he cared. He was happy to see how much fun Hannah was having with his family.

"See you Tuesday for the tree-trimming party," Joni said to Russell and Hannah as they walked to their cars. "Don't bother bringing ornaments. We have way too many as it is."

"We'll be there," Russell said before Hannah could reply. He didn't know whether she was going to beg off, but he didn't want to give her a chance. With his help she would be able to enjoy the holidays. Just look at how much fun she'd had tonight. She'd laughed more than he'd ever seen.

"Why did you say that?" Hannah asked once they were in his car and driving home. He blinked. Had he just thought of Hannah's house as his home? He tried not to read too much into it. After all, he was staying with her. Perhaps it was a Freudian slip. But even if he felt at home with Hannah, it didn't change the way things had to be between them. He believed that a man provided a home for his woman, not the other way around. She was established with a bright future while he was floundering. He wouldn't drag her onto his sinking ship.

"Well?" she prodded when he didn't answer.

"Well what?" He'd gotten so caught up in his thoughts that he'd lost track of the conversation.

"That we'd be at the tree-trimming party."

"Because as far as my family is concerned, you're my girlfriend. Surely you aren't going to back out now."

She frowned. "No. Of course not. I just didn't realize how much was involved."

"To be honest, I don't know myself. I've missed a lot of holidays with my family, so I'm not caught up on all the traditions. And with me being home for Christmas for the first time in a while, they've probably added a few extra get-togethers. But if you don't want to come to something my family has planned, just say so and I'll make an excuse for you." He'd hate it because he enjoyed being around her, but he didn't want her to be miserable.

She shook her head. "No. That's not fair to you. I'll be there."

"Thank you." The relief he felt at her answer was greater than the situation warranted, and that gave him pause. He was getting too involved here. It was as if he was forgetting the parameters they'd set in place. The relationship was starting to feel real.

He had to put a stop to these feelings. And fast.

Chapter Twelve

"If you don't mind, I'm going to leave for a couple of hours," Russell said.

Hannah swallowed the last of her clam chowder and set her spoon into her empty bowl. They'd just finished eating a late lunch and she'd been feeling relaxed. Though she'd seen her mother and sister at a distance last night while she was talking to another shop owner, she'd managed to avoid them. She'd prefer it if they'd been gone, but the fact that they weren't dogging her footsteps gave her hope. Perhaps they had accepted her no and would actually leave her alone.

The boutique had been a lot more manageable with her expanded staff. Russell still helped where he could. In fact, he was very popular with the ladies, who continued to seek out his opinion. Some of the older ladies had even begun to flirt with him, something Hannah felt was totally inappropriate and that made her uncomfortable. She'd apologized for their behavior but he'd only grinned and told her not to worry about it.

"They're just trying to make you jealous," he'd joke. She hated to admit that, as ridiculous as it sounded, they were succeeding. "But don't worry, I always tell them that I'm spoken for. Not to mention that they spend a lot of money."

That they did. Russell was definitely good for her bottom line.

She picked up their dishes and stood. "Sure."

"I'll be back in time to pick you up. Remember we're going caroling tonight."

She groaned. That was another of Mabel's bright ideas. She'd thought it would show the town that the business owners were a part of the community. Mabel had gotten together with Lex and Charlotte to schedule caroling over several days in the week before Christmas. The high school chorus had started things off, followed by the city employees and their families and various other groups. Today the business owners were supposed to sing for half an hour at the town square, then break into smaller groups to sing in residential neighborhoods. All told, it would be only about ninety minutes of her life.

But it was ninety minutes she would prefer to spend doing anything but that.

"I look forward to it," she lied. There was no sense in ruining it for him and her employees, who were excited about the night.

After spending time with Russell's family, Hannah had felt a flicker of Christmas spirit. She'd decided to fan the flame in the hopes that it would last. Before she could revert back to Scrooge status, she'd asked Russell to help her add a Nativity scene to her front yard. She'd had so much fun putting out the additional decorations that she'd agreed when he'd suggested they add candy canes and hang several strings of lights on the Fraser fir tree growing in the center of her lawn. Now her front yard looked festive.

Sadly, her Christmas spirit had waned since then; she hadn't retained the joy she'd felt. Clearly it was going to take more than a few decorations.

He winked and left.

The minute he was gone she missed him. If she didn't know better, she'd think she was lonely. Oh, this was getting to be ridiculous. Natasha, Talia and Alyssa were in the front of the shop, helping customers put together stylish outfits. Not only that, she'd worked alone in her boutique many times and had never felt lonely. The shop was her second home. She'd always been happy here. That shouldn't change just because Russell had come into her life. Their relationship was temporary. He'd be leaving soon and once more she'd be on her own. More to the point, their relationship wasn't even real. But that didn't stop the feelings from battering her from every side.

"Hannah," Alyssa said, coming into the break room. "There's someone here to see you."

"Okay." Hannah washed her hands and then followed her salesclerk out to the front of the store.

Valerie Danielson was standing near the counter. When she saw Hannah, she smiled. "I hope I'm not bothering you."

"Not at all. I'm glad to see you."

"Your clothes are lovely."

"Thank you. Are you looking for anything special?"

"Yes. Something for New Year's Eve. Every year Ross's fraternity has a fundraising party with dinner and dancing. I want a dress that's going to knock his socks off."

"We can totally do that."

Although Valerie had referred to herself as old the other day, she was youthful with a curvy figure. At about five foot seven, with smooth brown skin and a pretty face, she must have been a knockout in her day. Better than simply being pretty, she was kind.

Hannah led her to the party dresses. She had an idea of what would look good on Valerie, but unless she was specifically asked, she would keep her opinion to herself. She would treat Valerie as she would any other customer, letting her gravitate to the clothes she preferred. That way Hannah would get an idea of her taste and the colors and styles Valerie liked. If she was asked to help, she would already have an idea of Valerie's taste and be able to make a perfect match.

"Take a few minutes to look through here and see what you like. Hand me the items you want to try on and I'll get a fitting room started for you."

Valerie nodded and began removing dresses from the rack and holding them up to get a better look at them. Not wanting to hover, Hannah moved through the room, offering assistance to other shoppers.

A few minutes later, Valerie approached Hannah. She had five dresses draped over her arm. "I'd like to try these."

"Great. Let me see how they look on you."

Valerie nodded and went into the dressing room. When she stepped back out, she looked absolutely stunning in a gold dress with sequins down the side. Hannah took one look and knew they had a winner. The color was perfect with her skin tone and the style accentuated her figure. She didn't want to unduly influence Valerie's decision, but she did give two thumbs-up. Valerie tried on the other dresses, and even though she looked great in all of them, Hannah hoped she would choose the gold dress.

"I like the gold the most. What do you think?" Valerie asked.

"I was hoping you would choose that one. You look good in the others, but you look absolutely stunning in the gold."

"Now I just need a new purse and shoes to match."

"I don't sell shoes and purses, but I know where you can get some of the highest quality." Hannah gave her the name and directions to a store a block away.

"I was hoping to see Russell. Don't tell me you fired him."

Hannah was about to deny it when she saw the twinkle in Valerie's eyes and laughed instead. "You just missed him. He said he needed to go out for a while, but he promised to be back before closing." To take her caroling. How she managed not to frown at that thought was beyond her.

Last night, the women's guild—whoever they were—and their poor put-upon husbands had been caroling on her block. Hannah had wanted to pretend that she hadn't heard the doorbell, but Russell had answered the door before she could tell him not to. He'd stepped onto the porch and had provided the baritone that the unenthused husbands hadn't. Hannah hadn't wanted to raise the suspicions of her friends and neighbors who'd spotted her, so she had joined him. Surprisingly, a small part of her had enjoyed listening to the singing. Maybe her Christmas spirit was still trying to make a comeback.

"Right. You're going caroling tonight."

Hannah stifled a groan. "That's right. Of course, if you've made other plans, we can do that instead."

"I wouldn't dream of it. I know how important community involvement is to your business. And Russell loves to sing. He was a member of the high school chorus. He also had the leading role in the all-school musical his junior year. The head of the music department loved him. According to her, Russell made music cool and several other boys who looked up to him joined the chorus, too."

Hannah smiled, as her plans for escaping the night's festivities vanished before her eyes. "That sounds like Russell."

Valerie smiled proudly. "Of course, I'm not telling you anything about him that you haven't already figured out."

"That's true." Actually there was so much she didn't know about Russell and probably never would. But since she was supposed to be his girlfriend, she kept up the pretense.

Hannah rang up the sale for the dress and then placed it in a garment bag. Although she liked Russell's mother, Hannah breathed a sigh of relief when she left to find a purse and shoes.

"Meeting the parents," Natasha said.

Hannah looked at her young employee. "Yes."

"She seemed to like you, so that's always good."

Hannah agreed even though that was a problem. She was growing more attached to Russell and becoming more involved with his life and family. It was going to be painful when he walked away from her again.

Thinking about him no longer being a part of her life hurt more than it should. It was more painful than the memory of seeing her fiancé in bed with her sister. That didn't make sense. She'd been in love with Gerald, or at least the man she'd thought he was. She was only pretending to be in love with Russell. She didn't *actually* love him. Did she?

Hannah shoved all thoughts of love to the back of her mind and got back to work. She couldn't deal with that possibility now. Or ever. Russell wasn't in love with her so the entire train of thought was pointless. Thankfully there was a rush of customers, and even with her employees providing assistance, she was much too busy to think about her evolving feelings for Russell.

In fact, she barely thought of him the rest of

the day. He crossed her mind only a hundred or so times. But as she and the girls put on their coats before closing up, she checked her watch. Russell had promised to be back by now. Perhaps he'd forgotten about her.

A knock on the door stopped that negative train of thought before it could pick up speed. She opened it and there he was. He flashed her a devastating grin that sent butterflies zooming around her stomach. She really needed to get a grip before it was too late.

"Russell." Though she tried she couldn't keep the pleasure from her voice.

"Sorry to be late. It took longer than I'd expected."

"What did?"

He shook his head. "Nothing. Are you ready to go? We don't want to be late. They might start singing without us."

How wrong could a man be? "We were just getting ready to go now."

Russell and the girls exchanged smiles. Although he hadn't spent much time with them, they'd become very fond of him. They were all brimming with enthusiasm so she knew there wasn't the slightest chance that she would be able to get out of caroling. She might as well try to enjoy it. She didn't want to ruin the experience for them by being a Debbie Downer.

The evening was brisk and the sun had set. Before long stars would be twinkling in the darkening sky. Russell offered her his arm and she took it. He squeezed her hand and then side by side, they walked with the others to the main square. Mabel greeted them and then gave each of them a folder with the lyrics to the traditional carols. There hadn't been any rehearsals, but Hannah had been assured that they would be singing familiar songs.

A crowd gathered and Hannah felt a rush of nerves. She had many skills, but singing wasn't among them. Not that her lack of singing ability had kept her from belting out songs in the past. But there hadn't been an audience of her friends and neighbors then. There had to be at least one hundred people gathered and several more were running across the street to join them. Hannah didn't know how many people to expect because she hadn't attended the other nights.

She searched the crowd, hoping to spot an unfamiliar face. She'd feel less self-conscious serenading a stranger. She finally found a friendly-looking older woman chatting to kids who were probably her grandkids. That was whom she'd sing to.

"Relax," Russell whispered. His lips brushed her ear and she trembled. There were many words that could describe what his nearness made her feel—*aroused* and *tempted* being two—but *relaxed* wasn't one of them.

Kenneth Jenkins, the high school music teacher, spoke to Mabel, who nodded and then joined the other merchants. He then turned and spoke to the audience. "Welcome to the final night of Sweet Briar Sing-Along. Tonight's carolers are the owners and employees of many of the shops in Sweet Briar. They'll be leading the singing, but please feel free to join in. The more the merrier."

He announced the first song and, after a shaky start, the group began to sing with confidence and exuberance. Hannah stayed by Russell's side. His mother hadn't exaggerated his singing ability. His voice was clear and he had quite the range, hitting both the low and high notes.

After the third song, everyone in the audience was singing along and Hannah's nerves faded. The half hour passed quickly and before long they'd sung the last song. As the crowd dispersed, Kenneth spoke to the shop owners. There were approximately forty people and Kenneth proceeded to separate them into four groups. Each group was assigned a few blocks in a residential neighborhood where they would sing.

Russell and Hannah drove to their assigned area together and met up with their group ten minutes later. The singers buzzed with excitement as they rang the first doorbell. Hannah had to admit that singing to people who'd been unable to come downtown held appeal.

The door swung open and a girl of about ten grinned, then called over her shoulder. "Mom. The Christmas singers are here."

There was some commotion and then a small family gathered in the doorway. Because he was easily the best singer, Russell had been selected as the leader of the group. He started the song they'd all agreed upon and gradually the rest of them chimed in. When they finished, the family applauded and the mother shooed the children inside the house.

"You don't know how much this means to me and my family. My children really wanted to go downtown today, but my youngest is only a few weeks old and my husband works nights. I didn't want to bring the baby out with the crowds. Thank you so much for coming."

As they left, the mother's words stuck with Hannah. Although she hadn't wanted to participate initially, she now realized that it hadn't been about her. It was about bringing joy to someone else. She doubted she would personally experience the joy she'd once felt at Christmas, but the possibility that she could bring happiness to someone else made her discomfort worthwhile.

Hannah sang with more exuberance at the next houses. Each person who opened the door was happy to see the carolers. By the time they were finished singing and had said good-night, Hannah was feeling better than she had since the season started. Not that she wasn't still counting the minutes until it was over. She was. But for the moment, she'd felt a small spark of joy inside her.

When the carolers finished, they said good night and hopped in their cars.

Hannah was glad the night was over. Tonight may have turned out better than she'd expected, but being outwardly cheerful was emotionally exhausting. It would be good to be home with Russell, the one person who understood how she felt about Christmas. He respected her feelings and didn't try to force her to act differently. She could be herself when she was with him.

It felt good to be understood.

They pulled in front of her house. The timer had turned on the Christmas lights. She and Russell had added the candy canes and Nativity scene, and the house helped her feel more of the Christmas spirit than she had in a while. Perhaps her love of Christmas wasn't truly gone.

They climbed the stairs and then she unlocked the door. Russell suddenly seemed excited and nervous. He was smiling broadly as if he knew a great secret and she wondered what was up. She stepped inside and the scent of pine assaulted her. She jerked her head around. A gigantic Christmas tree was standing beside her unlit fireplace and every ornament on the face of the earth dangled from the tree.

So much for Russell understanding how she felt about Christmas. Clearly she'd been wrong. He didn't get it. He was just like everyone else. He wanted her to jump into the holiday season in order to make him comfortable—even if she had to fake it.

Well, she'd put on a happy face for the last time. She was going to be true to herself.

She looked at Russell, letting the anger and disappointment show in her expression. *"What is that tree doing in my house?"*

Russell looked at the fury on Hannah's face, heard the pain in her voice, and knew he'd made a tactical error. Somehow or another he'd misinterpreted her words and actions of the past days. When she'd asked him to help her add decorations on her lawn and to decorate the tree, he'd taken that as a sign that she'd begun to put the past behind her. She'd also seemed to enjoy the carolers the other day. He'd thought she was reclaiming her love of Christmas and he was simply going along with her. Clearly he'd made the biggest mistake of his life. He'd gotten so wrapped up in wanting to make her happy that he'd misread everything. He'd hurt her, which was the last thing he'd wanted to do.

"I told you I didn't want a tree."

"I remember."

"Then why did you do this?"

"I thought you had changed your mind." The words sounded lame to him, but they were true.

"What made you think that?"

"A few things. You added more decorations outside. I've heard you singing along to some of the music at the shop, something you hadn't done before."

"And from that you decided that I wanted a tree?"

She waved her hands in aggravation. She was so annoyed that she hadn't removed her coat. He reached for her and she snatched her arm away. "I was just going to help you take off your coat."

"I don't need your help. I can take care of myself. See?" She snatched off her coat and dropped it onto a chair. "I don't have a tree because I don't want one. If I did, I would have gotten one. I'm capable of doing that, too."

She paced the room in anger. Rather than try to pacify her, he just let her speak.

"I thought you were different. I thought you were better."

"Than what?"

"Than everybody else. You know Gerald cheated

on me. Before a day had even passed, my mother told me to get over it. I always knew she'd loved Dinah more, but even so I couldn't believe she could say something so unfeeling to me. My fiancé had cheated on me with my sister and she thought I should just move on. Act like it had never happened. Pretend like I had never loved him. But then, that's the way she looked at relationships. They weren't meant to last. Believing otherwise was just stupid on my part so I deserved the heartache that I got. She told me I should learn from it."

"Are you really comparing me to your mother? When have I ever told you to get over it? When have I ever told you it was time to move on? Those words have never come out of my mouth and they never will."

"You don't need to say the words. Your actions are speaking loudly for you."

"I bought you a tree." He kept his voice level—but barely. It wouldn't help for both of them to yell. He was upset, but of the two, she had more of a reason.

"Yes. Because in your mind I need one. I need to give the outward appearance of celebrating in order to make *you* happy. *You* need me to smile and be filled with cheer. Not for myself, but for you. For your own comfort."

"You are so wrong, Hannah."

"Am I?"

He nodded. "Yes, I want you to enjoy the holidays, but that's so you'll be happy, not so that I will."

"I am happy."

"Really? Because you don't seem happy. It looks to me that you're counting the minutes until Christmas is over. If there's any Christmas spirit inside you, it's buried way down deep."

"That's what I'm talking about. Why do I need Christmas spirit? You want me to put on a happy face to convince you that I'm happy. You want me to do what you want me to do. You want me to say the lines in the script that you've written. I'm not interested in playing a role. I want to live my life."

He didn't mention that she was already playing a role. They both were.

"Are you still in love with Gerald?" That question came out of nowhere, taking him by surprise. But suddenly he needed to know. Maybe she still harbored feelings for her former fiancé, which would explain why she didn't have any Christmas spirit. Perhaps she still wanted to be with him and celebrating Christmas was one more reminder that he'd be spending the holidays with someone else.

"Have you lost your mind?"

Maybe. Probably. He might not be crazy, but he was definitely jealous. "I notice you didn't answer the question."

"No. I am not still in love with Gerald. I can't believe you asked me that."

Relief made him weak. He tried to deny that was what he felt, but he wasn't successful. It shouldn't matter to him whether she still had feelings for her former fiancé. Sure, he was happy that she wasn't still hung up on that worthless snake, but the relief wasn't for her. It was for himself. It was as if he had a vested interest in her emotions and any feelings she had for the other man were a threat to him. He shook his head. That didn't make sense. He wasn't in love with Hannah. Was he? No. They were just pretending.

"So you're calling me a liar?" Her voice was shocked and hurt.

"What? I didn't say a word."

"You shook your head."

"That wasn't at you."

"I'm the only other person here." She snatched her coat and for a minute he thought she was going to leave. Instead she hung it on the old-fashioned coat rack near the front door. "You know, rather than talk about me, why don't we talk about you. You criticize me for being stuck in the past, but you're no different."

"I'm not living in the past."

"Aren't you? How many times have you told me that you're a soldier in the United States Army?"

The way she emphasized the last words grated on him. "I am."

"For how much longer? You are in the process of retiring. Then what will you be? How will you define yourself then if not as a soldier? Everything you are is wrapped up in your job."

"I don't need this." He stormed to the stairs. Before he reached them, he felt his arm being pulled.

She stepped in front of him. "Oh, you can dish it out, but you can't take it. You just need to keep up the image. Mr. Stoic Soldier. Mr. Heroic Soldier. You talk about me but from where I stand you're living in the past."

"Me? What about you? You may not still be in love with that jerk, but you're letting him keep you from enjoying yourself. You've learned your mother's lessons very well. Image above everything."

She gasped and let go of his arm. Pain covered her face and he wanted to call the words back. But he couldn't. Once words were spoken, there was no taking them back.

"I'm done. I'm going to bed." She ran from the room and the only thing he could do was watch her go.

When he was alone, he dropped onto the sofa and closed his eyes. That was not the way he'd expected the night to go. He'd thought that Hannah would be pleased by the tree and recognize the feelings behind his gesture. He'd hoped to replace bad memories with good ones. Instead he'd given her another reason to wish the season away.

"Way to go, soldier," he muttered to himself. He froze. Frowned. Was that really how he thought of himself? Was his identity so wrapped up with being a soldier that he couldn't picture himself as a man if he no longer wore the uniform? That was crazy. Sure, he thought of himself as a soldier. He'd been in the army over half his life. The turmoil he felt wasn't at no longer being a soldier. It was a result of not knowing where to go next.

But really, was that any different from what Hannah felt? She was focused on the past and didn't know how to move on from the pain. But it wasn't up to him to help her to get over her pain, no matter how much he wanted to. She had to do things her way.

They weren't really involved. She wasn't his real girlfriend. After tonight, she might not even be his friend.

He'd overstepped, forgetting his mission. When he'd decided to be her fake boyfriend, it was to protect her feelings and soothe her damaged ego. He'd seen how deflated she'd been as her sister had insulted her. And he'd just done the same thing. His intent was totally different—he wanted her to feel good about herself—but the result had been the same.

Rising, he walked to the tree and removed a glass angel. He wrapped it in tissue paper and then set it in the ornament storage case he'd purchased. Putting up the tree had been infinitely more fun than taking it down would be. There was only the memory of her anger—and pain. But he knew she wouldn't want to see the tree in the morning. If it took all night, he was going to remove every trace of it.

When he'd removed the last ornament, Russell dragged the now bare tree into the backyard. He didn't know what to do with it. It was a good tree—the best they'd had on the lot in Willow Creek—and he didn't want to let it go to waste. Lex was the mayor. Maybe he knew of a family in need of a tree.

He went back inside and straight to the guest room. He knew he wouldn't be able to sleep, but more than anything he wanted this day to be over.

Chapter Thirteen

Hannah forced a smile all the while wishing this lunch with her friends would end. Sadly, the end was nowhere in sight. They'd only just finished eating and were about to open their gifts. She generally enjoyed the food served at Marconi's restaurant, but she'd barely managed to choke down enough of her manicotti to keep her friends from becoming suspicious. As it was, she'd been the recipient of a couple of puzzled looks. Great. Just what she didn't need. Perhaps she shouldn't have turned down the waiter's offer of tiramisu, her usual dessert of choice.

She hadn't slept a wink last night. As a person

who preferred peace to arguing, she'd grown un-easy whenever she thought of how she'd behaved. She hated being angry with Russell and was un-comfortable with the distance between them. But she was also too hurt and disappointed in him to forgive him. Besides, he hadn't apologized. She wasn't the type to grant absolution to someone who hadn't sought it.

But that was only part of the reason she'd tossed and turned all night. The angry words that had come spewing out of her mouth had repeated over and over in her brain followed by the image of the shock and pain in Russell's eyes. Hurt that she'd caused.

She'd known he was having trouble accepting the fact that although he was still a young man, he was no longer able to perform the job he loved. When he'd confided that he'd improved as much as he would and that he would be forced to retire, he'd trusted her. She'd betrayed that trust. The first time they disagreed, she'd thrown his words back into his face, hurting him. Her pain wasn't an excuse. She owed him an apology, too.

But how could she apologize and mean it when her heart still ached? She wouldn't be in this pre-dicament if she'd lived up to her motto of thinking before speaking. But yesterday she'd been ruled by her emotions and unable to consider her words. For better or worse, Russell had the ability to make her feel deeply. He reached her on a level that no one else ever had.

She must have eventually dozed off from exhaustion because she overslept and didn't have time to do much more than shower and get dressed for work this morning. As she'd descended the stairs, she'd noticed that there wasn't the delicious aroma of breakfast that had greeted her most mornings since Russell had come to stay with her. Maybe he'd overslept, too. Or perhaps he'd decided that he didn't want to stay with her any longer and had gone back to the Sunrise B&B. Clearly he hadn't gone to stay with Joni or Brandon because either Joni or Arden would have said something. Her heart ached at the thought. She couldn't decide if the pain was a result of worrying if Russell would run into her family or at the thought that he had left her.

She'd been out the front door when she'd realized that she hadn't smelled pine, either. Turning, her eyes went to the spot by the fireplace where Russell had put up the tree. The tree had been gone and the chair that he'd moved beside the window was now in its rightful place. The relief Hannah had expected to feel had never come. Instead there'd been shame. She'd taken his kind gesture and thrown it back into his teeth with a vengeance.

"Are we ready to exchange gifts?" Charlotte asked, pulling Hannah back to the present.

"I am," Hannah said, and the rest of the women chimed in. She wanted to get this over with so she could go back to the boutique and sulk in private. Of course, there wasn't much privacy at the shop these days. Her salesclerks would be there taking care of the ever-present shoppers. Even so, they weren't as observant as Hannah's friends, so they wouldn't pick up on her mood as easily.

The women had placed their wrapped boxes and gift bags on the two empty chairs at their table. Charlotte was the closest and she volunteered to distribute the packages. Over the past week, each Secret Santa had left two small gifts for the person whose name she'd drawn. Hannah had received a mug and a picture frame. There was much laughter as Hannah and her friends tried to guess their Secret Santas. Hannah's heart lifted a little bit as she watched her friends open their presents. She hoped Raven Reynolds-Cordero, one of her friends, liked the gift she'd gotten for her.

Joni and Arden had already opened their gifts and now it was Hannah's turn.

"It's heavier than it looks," Charlotte said, handing her a gaily wrapped box. It was about a foot tall and a foot and half wide.

"Thanks." Hannah's anticipation grew. She couldn't imagine what was inside. Rather than tear the paper off with abandon, she slowly unwrapped the ribbon, then removed the bow. Next she slid her fingernail below the tape holding the paper in place, and moved the paper inch by inch.

"You're killing me here," Arden whined. She'd shredded the wrapping on her gift in seconds. But then, she had a loving husband and extended family who would be showering her with gifts. This would be the only Christmas gift Hannah received this year and she wanted to make the moment last.

"Patience is a virtue," Hannah teased. Nevertheless, she picked up the pace. After she'd removed the last bit of tape, she pulled open the paper and gasped. She'd received a spectacular painting and knew immediately who it was from. "Oh my goodness. This is beautiful. Thank you so much."

"You're welcome," Carmen said.

Hannah held up the painting so everyone else could see. Carmen Shields-Knight was a famous artist. Her work was exquisite and sold for amounts way out of Hannah's price range. "I know exactly where I'm going to hang this. I've been looking for the right picture to hang over my fireplace, but nothing quite fit."

Carmen smiled. "That's exactly what I was thinking when I was working on it."

"I think I've gotten the best present of all," Hannah said. She darted around the table and gave her friend a hug. Who needed a sister when she had such good friends in Sweet Briar?

Charlotte continued to pass out gifts. Everyone said that their gifts were perfect. Hannah held her breath as Charlotte gave the gift Hannah had selected to Raven. She'd worried for days over what to get her friend, wanting to get something that she would like. She just hoped Raven was as pleased with her present as Hannah was with her painting.

Her stomach bunched up in knots as Raven tore the paper from the box. Raven was a rancher's wife, but she worked the ranch just as much as her husband, Donovan. A tomboy, Raven lived in jeans and boots.

"This is perfect," Raven exclaimed, much to Hannah's relief. She'd had the jewelry designed especially for Raven. "I love these earrings and bracelet." She held one of the delicate turquoise and silver earrings to her ear.

"But will you wear them?" Hannah asked. The only jewelry Hannah had seen Raven wear was her wedding band and a bracelet that she never took off.

"Absolutely. They're exquisite. Donovan and I are going out for New Year's Eve. Now I have jewelry, if nothing else."

"Stop by the shop and I'll help you find the right dress."

"A dress by the designer to the stars," Raven joked. "I know I'll be the belle of the ball."

"So you'll design a dress for strangers, but not

for your own sister. Do your friends know how petty you are?" Dinah's angry voice tore through Hannah's enjoyment and silenced the voices of her friends.

Hannah cringed and looked over her shoulder. Eleanor and Dinah stood side by side, clearly ready for battle. How had they found her? Were they stalking her? But then, did it matter? They were here now.

It had been bad enough having her dirty laundry aired out in front of Russell. She'd been embarrassed then, but this was worse. She and Russell hadn't known each other very long when he'd found out the truth, so he hadn't had a reason to expect her to share her past with him. But these were her closest friends. They'd celebrated the best times and commiserated during the worst of times. Yet she'd hidden a great deal of herself from them. Just what did that say about their friendship? About her? Did she care more about upholding her image than having deep, true friendships that were the result of vulnerability and trust?

Hannah felt a hand on hers and glanced up. Joni nodded and gave her an encouraging smile. Hannah looked at her other friends. They all gave her signals of support. She wasn't alone.

Hannah stood, forcing her sister and mother to take several steps back. Apparently this was their latest strategy. If they thought humiliating her in front of her friends would get her to capitulate, they were mistaken. Her mother's outrageous behavior had generally won her bigger divorce settlements from husbands who'd preferred to keep their bad choice of a spouse a secret. Maybe that worked for them. But it didn't work for Hannah. She hadn't chosen her mother or sister. It had been the luck of the draw. Bad luck at that.

"Nothing to say?" Dinah said. "You don't want your friends to know the kind of person you are. Maybe I'll let them know that you won't design your own sister's wedding gown."

Hannah breathed slowly as Russell's words came back to her. He was right. She wasn't responsible for her mother and sister's behavior. That was on them. And she was tired of letting them control her life. Tired of running and hiding who she was. Crossing her arms over her chest, she smiled. She noticed the defiance in Dinah's eyes change to doubt. "Whatever floats your boat. But when you tell everyone how wrong I am not to design your wedding dress, don't forget to mention the reason why I won't. Tell everyone how you slept with my fiancé a week before the wedding. Tell them how you went on what was supposed to be my honeymoon without giving me a second thought. Don't leave out a detail. And when you're done and our dirty laundry is hanging from one end of town to the other, I still won't design a dress for you."

Hannah looked past her sister to her mother. Eleanor was unusually silent and looking slightly uncomfortable. Was it finally starting to click with her that there was no tactic they could come up with that would get Hannah to design a dress for Dinah? Did she finally get the message that Hannah would never allow them to be a part of her life with access to her wealthy friends? Had she figured out that creating a scene would only make her look bad? Or had she finally figured out that Hannah didn't give a flying fig about either of them? "And Mother, you be sure to tell them about your many marriages. How each one was a stepping-stone into high society and a way to get more money."

"Maybe we should talk about this in private," Eleanor said. Yep. It had finally occurred to her that she wasn't going to win this fight and she was trying to salvage what was left of her carefully constructed image.

"Why? This is what you've been threatening to do. You're the ones who wanted to blackmail me into designing a dress for Dinah. Don't back out now when your plan isn't working. This was your main card. Or was it your last card?"

"I just thought designing a dress for your sister would give you the opportunity to rebuild your relationship. If I was wrong to push, please forgive me. But as a mother, it hurts to see my only two children at odds. Surely you can understand that."

So now Eleanor was the poor, heartbroken mother. "I understand everything perfectly well. Now, how about you leave me alone as you have for the past three years and I'll do the same."

Eleanor huffed. Then, realizing she'd played the last card in her hand, she turned and stormed from the restaurant, Dinah right behind her.

Hannah looked at her friends. "Sorry about that. I guess I should explain why I've never mentioned having a family."

"You don't owe us an apology," Arden said. "Or anything else for that matter."

Hannah sat back down. "Thank you."

"Trust me, we all have pasts and people we wish we never met. Lucky for us, none of those people are members of our own families," Joni said.

"You can say that again," Arden said. "The stories I could tell you."

Hannah breathed out a relieved breath. What could have been a horribly embarrassing moment passed with the women recounting stories of relationships gone bad. And to think, she'd actually been embarrassed for her mother and sister to find out she hadn't had a boyfriend.

But she had to admit that at the time she'd been grateful for Russell's interference. He'd stepped in and saved her pride, asking nothing in return. True, she'd pretended to be his girlfriend in order to keep his parents from nagging him about settling down. Now that she'd met them, she wondered if he'd actually needed her for that. His parents were wonderful and supportive of their children. She didn't think they would ever pressure him to settle down until he'd found the right woman.

So why had he asked her to pretend? Had he been mistaken about how his parents would act? Or had he simply been trying to make things more equal between them? Had that been another example of him trying once more to save her pride? Whatever his reason, she'd enjoyed being his pretend girlfriend. She'd had the best time with him whether they were at his family gatherings, on dates or alone in her home. Somewhere along the line she'd stopped thinking of herself as Russell's pretend girlfriend and had begun to think of herself as his *girlfriend*.

She didn't know when it happened, but the relationship felt real. The change had been so subtle. The emotions had sneaked up on her so slowly that she hadn't noticed until it was too late. That's why she'd been so angry and hurt yesterday. She cared for him and his actions affected her deeply.

She'd fallen in love with Russell. And she'd chased him out of her life.

* * *

Russell was doing his best to keep a low profile. After last night's disaster, he'd thought it best to keep his distance from Hannah, so he'd stayed in his room until he'd heard her leave for work this morning. Then he'd paced the house, trying to figure out how he could fix things between them. When nothing came to mind, he'd pulled on his workout clothes and gone for a run.

Although he didn't want to, he was going to have to stay with Brandon and Arden. It had been too late to go over after he'd taken down the tree last night. And because her family was still in town, returning to the B&B was out of the question. He wouldn't risk running into them and causing Hannah even more grief.

He'd never seen her so angry and wanted to give her time to cool off. Though he was no longer upset, he was still stinging from her words.

That was the bad thing about not having had serious relationships in the past. There were so many things he didn't know—like how to reconcile after a fight. He imagined chocolate and flowers would play a part, but how much chocolate and what type of flowers? Should he go to the boutique or should he give her space? And how much space? How much time should he let pass before approaching Hannah to talk things through? Too little time and she'd think he wasn't taking her feelings seriously. Too much time and she'd believe he was indifferent. It was a delicate dance and he didn't know the steps.

Since his past involvement had been superficial, lasting only while both parties were having fun, he'd never reached this point in a relationship. Though he'd been fond of the other women, he'd never cared as deeply for them as he did for Hannah. None of this had mattered because he hadn't loved them.

Russell stumbled to a screeching stop and nearly lost his balance. Had he just thought that he loved Hannah? And not love as in a friend but love as in a woman. His woman. That couldn't be right. This was a pretend relationship. One with rules and an end date. He spotted a bench a few feet away so he jogged over and sat down. After a thought like that, he needed to get off his feet.

He wiped his forehead and waited for the panic and denial to set in. When neither feeling came, he relaxed. What if he was in love with Hannah? Would that be so awful? She was a wonderful woman. She had a kind heart and a generous spirit. He enjoyed being with her and never tired of her company.

Yet he'd hurt her badly. Perhaps irrevocably. For the first time, losing his career wasn't the worst thing that could happen to him. Losing Hannah was.

He rubbed his aching knee. The knee that although surgically repaired would keep him from returning to the army. He felt sad but he wasn't devastated. Even when he'd been undergoing therapy, a part of him had always known he wouldn't be able to regain his strength. His career had ended sooner than he'd planned, but he could find solace in knowing that he'd given it his all. It was time for him to embrace his new reality. Of course that new reality wasn't what he'd expected it to be. He was still unsure what his future held. But one thing was certain. He wanted Hannah to be a part of his life. He just needed to figure out how to fix things between them. But first he had to find a way to convince her to forgive him.

He would have liked to take her out to dinner tonight, or better yet cook dinner for her so they could be alone, but he couldn't.

Tonight was the town Christmas party and he'd committed to playing Santa Claus. He couldn't just make an appearance and then leave. He had to pose for pictures with the little ones and then hand out gifts, which meant he'd have to be there from the beginning to the very end.

If only he could have convinced Hannah to play Mrs. Claus. Then he would have been guaranteed the opportunity to see her in a few hours. They might have been able to talk things through. And who knew, maybe being surrounded by a bunch of excited kids might have helped her catch the Christmas spirit.

He checked his watch. It was getting late. He stood and began to jog back to Hannah's house. His route took him past the Sunrise B&B. The door opened and Hannah's mother stomped down the stairs, then tapped her foot on the sidewalk in obvious irritation. Not wanting to be seen—although he didn't know why it mattered—he stepped behind an evergreen tree. He doubted that he was totally obscured, but it was the best he could do, so he stood still and hoped for the best.

Eleanor turned and called up the stairs. "Would you hurry up? I don't want to spend another minute in this stupid town."

"I'm coming," Dinah snapped as she descended the stairs, dragging two designer suitcases behind her. "And I don't know why you're mad at me. You're the one who wanted to come here, not me."

"Because it's your fault that things didn't work out. If you wouldn't have been so antagonistic to her, she might have made that dress for you. Then you would have gotten some publicity. Who knows where that would have led or who we could have met. We had the opportunity to make some connections and you blew it. Now we're right back where we started."

Dinah huffed and rolled her eyes.

Gerald emerged from the B&B, lugging even

more suitcases. He clicked the button on his key fob and the trunk of their car unlocked. Dinah yanked it open, then threw her luggage inside. Gerald approached her and she stepped away from him. Trouble in paradise? Russell wasn't petty by nature, but a part of him wished them the absolute worst in life. They'd been indifferent to the pain they'd caused Hannah. In his opinion, they didn't deserve to be happy. At least not until Hannah was.

As he watched the car pull away from the curb, he wondered what had happened to make them leave town so suddenly. The last he'd known, they'd been trying to convince Hannah to design Dinah's dress and somehow weasel their way into her life. Apparently she must have finally gotten them to understand that she wasn't interested in establishing a relationship with them.

Under other circumstances, he'd be thrilled that the three of them were no longer going to be around. But their absence made his position precarious. With them gone, Hannah no longer needed to pretend she and Russell were in love. True, she'd agreed to keep up the pretense while his parents were in town, but they would be leaving the day after Christmas. Four days from now. That didn't give him much time.

This was such a mess. He could continue to try to figure it out on his own or he could swallow his pride and seek the advice of an expert. He pulled out his phone and quickly dialed his father's number.

His parents had perfected the art of being married. After forty years together, they could teach a master class on making a relationship work.

His parents agreed to meet him for an early dinner at Mabel's Diner. He made a quick trip home to shower and change and was sitting at a booth near the back when they arrived. Standing, he waved to get their attention. They smiled and made their way through the restaurant. Russell noticed that his father kept his hand on his mother's waist as they walked. It was a little thing, but it showed the affection between his parents.

That's what Russell wanted. He wanted to love a woman so completely that making physical contact with her was as natural as breathing. He wanted to share the inside jokes and do the things that turned everyday events into special occasions.

He kissed his mother's cheek and gave his father a hug. Once they were seated and had ordered, he got to the point. "I need your advice."

His parents exchanged a glance. "What's wrong?" his father asked. Apparently he was the designated spokesperson.

"Everything. My career. My relationship. My future." He hadn't planned to talk about his injury but suddenly he found himself telling them about his knee. "Rehab helped, but I'm never going to be able to rejoin my unit. Right now the army is processing my retirement papers."

"Did you give it your best?" his father asked.

"Yes."

"I know how much being a soldier means to you. Finding a career that suits you makes it much more than a job. It becomes part of you. Your identity."

"I can function in society, so I know I should feel grateful that it wasn't worse. But it feels like..."

"Like someone tore out your heart?" Valerie said softly.

He nodded. "For the longest time, I couldn't figure out who I would be if I wasn't a soldier."

"And now?"

"It's taken me some time, but I finally know that I'm still the same man I was. On the inside anyway. I'm still Russell Danielson, your son and Joni and Brandon's brother." Hannah had helped him to see that.

"I noticed you didn't mention Hannah," his father said.

"Don't tell me things didn't work out with her," his mother said sadly. "I really like her."

Russell poked at his meal with his fork. He'd taken a few bites of his meat loaf and mashed potatoes when the waitress had first brought it, but he'd discovered that despite the fact that he hadn't eaten yet today, he didn't have much of an appetite. "I was kind of an idiot and hurt her. I'm looking for advice on how to make it better."

He quickly explained the debacle with the Christmas tree. "What should I do?"

"Apologize," his parents said in unison.

"I know that. And I will. But even if she forgives me, I don't have anything to offer her. No career. No future."

"You might not have a career right now, but you do have a future. You just have to figure out a way to move forward. That may take time, but you'll face it with the same strength as you've faced any other difficulty that's come your way," his father said.

"And with Hannah by your side, you'll be able to live your truth," his mother added.

The words *truth* and *Hannah* in the same sentence struck Russell in the gut. There was no reason to continue the farce. Hannah's family and her former fiancé had just left town. And honestly, he didn't need to lie to his parents about his feelings for Hannah. Not anymore. They were as solid as this table.

"Well, there's something I need to tell you about that."

"What now?"

He quickly explained the situation between

Hannah and her family that had set everything in motion.

"I understand pretending for them, but why did you lie to us?"

"We didn't want to put you in a position to cover for us. Besides, the fewer people who know a secret, the easier it is to keep."

"Are they still in town? I'd like to give them a piece of my mind," his mother said, offended on Hannah's behalf.

"Down, tiger," his father joked, patting Valerie's hand. "She has Russell to help her fight her battles."

"That's right," Russell quickly agreed. "Our relationship might have started off as a way to protect her pride, but it's not pretend now. I want things to work out between us."

"So why are you telling us instead of her?"

"I'm going to. I was just hoping to have something to offer her."

"I've seen the way Hannah looks at you," his mother said. "She lights up when you're around. Trust me, all she wants is you."

Russell's heart skipped a beat. "I hope you're right."

His mother smiled. "When have I ever been wrong?"

Russell pondered that a second. Never. His appetite suddenly returned and he picked up his fork and began to eat. His mother was right. He and Hannah belonged together. Once they worked through this bump in the road, they could focus on their future.

He just hoped she agreed.

Chapter Fourteen

Hannah closed and locked the door of the boutique and stepped onto the sidewalk. The day had been busy but luckily business had tapered off as closing time neared, giving her and her employees time to get the store ready for tomorrow. As she'd done earlier in the day at lunch with her friends, she'd managed to keep up a good front. She'd smiled and joked with the girls, never letting them see just how heartbroken she was. Russell hadn't shown up today—not that she'd expected him to. They'd said so many things in anger that couldn't be taken back, and they hadn't cleared the air yet. Perhaps it had been a mistake to leave without talking to him. But since there was no going backward, she could only go forward.

Over the years, she'd heard many people say not to go to bed angry with a person you loved. Not that she and Russell were in love. They weren't. She might be in love with him, but at this point she was uncertain of his feelings. She was hopeful, but hope wasn't fact.

But she was certain that their relationship was no longer strictly pretend, either. Although it hadn't progressed to the point that they'd led people to believe, they could eventually get to that point—if he was interested in continuing to see her. Even though he hadn't kept in touch with her when he'd left this past summer, she was the first person he'd come to see the minute he'd gotten to town. Her heart sped up as she recalled seeing his unopened luggage in his room at the B&B. That fact had seemed inconsequential at the time, but now it took on new meaning. He'd been so anxious to see her that he hadn't bothered to unpack.

Looking back, it was clear that they'd been working their way to a real relationship. So they'd hit a bump in the road. It happened to everyone. No doubt there would be other bumps in the future. Was she going to let one disagreement keep her from being with the man she loved? No. Her relationship with Russell was worth fighting for.

They needed to talk. It was time for them to put

their cards on the table and see what they held. She believed Russell cared for her. Even though she hadn't wanted a Christmas tree, she had to admit that it had been given with the best intentions. He'd only been trying to make her happy.

She began walking to her car and then paused. He wasn't going to be at her house. Tonight he was playing Santa Claus at the town Christmas party. In about thirty minutes he'd be setting kids on his lap while a photographer snapped pictures. Later he'd hand out gifts to the kids. She would just have to wait until he got home later to talk to him. The party would be over in a few hours. Surely anything she had to say would be just as true in a few hours as it was now.

But was that good enough? She thought of what Russell had said to her. How she had let Gerald and Dinah's betrayal keep her from enjoying Christmas. Although she'd immediately denied it, she was coming to believe that he might have been right.

Hannah used to love everything about Christmas. She'd loved the songs and the decorations. The cookies and the cakes and parties. The television specials and movies she'd rewatched every year even though she knew every word of dialogue. She'd loved the anticipation that had flavored the air. The season was so happy and filled with hope. From the time she'd been a child, she'd looked forward to Christmas.

That joy had vanished when she'd caught Dinah and Gerald together. It was understandable that she hadn't wanted to celebrate Christmas that year. After all, her hopes and dreams had been dashed a week earlier. It was even understandable that she hadn't been in the Christmas spirit the following year.

But at some point, she'd let the dreariness overtake her. She'd gotten used to being miserable during the Christmas season. It was as if that misery had become her new tradition. Rather than hang lights over her windows, decorate her tree and bake cookies, she'd bah-humbugged her way from the day after Thanksgiving until the day after Christmas. She shook her head as she realized how she'd let their behavior keep her from enjoying her life. Heck, she'd willingly become Ebenezer Scrooge. Thankfully she hadn't needed to be visited by three spirits before she came to her senses.

No, it had taken only one man to help her to see the light. So what was she going to do? The answer was easy. She was going to do the wise thing. She was going to walk in the light.

The Christmas party was being held at the youth center, so that's where she was going. She arrived a few minutes before the party started. The parking lot was filling with cars as families came to celebrate. Several people were on their way inside and she hopped out of her car and joined them. The building had been decorated with hundreds if not thousands of lights. It looked like something she might see at the North Pole. She loved it.

She stepped inside. Energy filled the space as little kids raced around. Some of the preteens tried to play it cool, as if they were too old to care about Santa and this party, but she read the excitement in their eyes. The toddler set might not have understood everything, but they knew about Santa and they'd definitely been clued in on presents he'd bring with him.

Several teenagers wearing elf costumes walked around, talking to parents and getting the names and ages of their kids. There had been a fundraiser earlier in the year to raise money to buy Christmas gifts for the children in addition to the coloring books and candy canes that one of Santa's helpers would give them. Although Sweet Briar was a middle-class to upper-middle-class town, there were families who struggled to pay for extras. The gifts the kids received tonight would be welcome additions to the ones they would receive on Christmas morning.

Hannah saw Alyssa, who was dressed as an elf, and approached her. "Hi. You look so cute."

Alyssa grinned and struck a pose. "Thanks.

I thought it was an original design. Imagine my surprise when I noticed that everyone was wearing this same outfit."

Hannah laughed at the joke. "Maybe, but I'm sure none of them look as good as you. So where is Santa set up?"

"The party's going to be in the gym. Right now he's hiding in the art room so the kids won't see him before he makes his grand entrance. I'm sure he won't mind if you pop in and say hello."

An idea began to form and Hannah shook her head. "Do you know who's playing Mrs. Santa?"

"Joni. She's around here someplace."

"In costume?"

"No. She's talking to the kids and making sure that they see her. She thinks that if they see her now, they won't suspect that she's actually Mrs. Claus when they see her later." Alyssa shook her head as if she thought that was the most ridiculous thing ever. Hannah had to agree. As director, Joni was the face of the youth center. The kids saw her every day and would easily recognize her in her costume.

"I'll find her. See you later."

It didn't take Hannah long to locate Joni. She was surrounded by a group of kids who were talking a mile a minute. When Joni saw Hannah, her eyes widened and then she smiled and disentangled herself from the kids.

"I didn't expect to see you here," Joni said. Obviously her friend recalled how she'd reacted at dinner that night.

"I'm a bit surprised myself."

"Are you looking for Russell?"

"No. Actually, I'm looking for you."

"Well, you found me. I have a couple of minutes before I need to change."

"That's what I wanted to talk to you about. Can we go into your office?"

"Sure."

They passed many kids who'd wanted to hug Joni or just say hello, so it took a few minutes to get there.

Once they were inside, Joni sat down and unzipped her boots. "Do you mind if I get changed while we talk? I need to meet up with Santa so we can get the party started."

"Actually I do."

"Do what?"

"I mind."

Joni's brow wrinkled in obvious confusion, which wasn't surprising. Hannah wasn't making sense. She inhaled and decided to try again, starting at the beginning. "I know I said that I didn't want to play Mrs. Claus but I've changed my mind. Unless your heart is set on being the jolly old elf's wife, I'd like to do it."

"That's fine by me. And I know that Russell would rather have you as his wife."

Hannah's heart leaped at the word *wife*. There was a lot to straighten out and talk through before she and Russell reached that point in their relationship. First she needed to know if he loved her. Though it was painful to admit, it was possible that he didn't think of her as anything more than a friend. After all, that's how he'd consistently referred to her.

But even as that thought hit her, she mentally shoved it aside. She knew Russell cared about her as more than a friend. His actions proved that. Whether his feelings were as deep as hers, or whether they needed time to grow, was another story. But she wasn't in any hurry. They had lots of time for their relationship to blossom.

"Thanks."

"You get changed and I'll let him know about the switch."

Joni started to leave but Hannah grabbed her arm. "Don't. I want to surprise him."

"Is that right?" Joni sat down. She was clearly curious and Hannah knew she was dying to ask a bunch of questions. In the past she would have. Hannah wondered if Joni's reticence was a result of what had happened at today's lunch. It had become clear to Joni and all of Hannah's friends just how much she'd withheld from them. Hannah had unintentionally built invisible walls between herself and her closest friends. If the walls were going to fall down, Hannah had to start dismantling them.

"We kind of had a fight," Hannah said. She was no longer concerned about keeping up appearances. Reality was better than pretense any day. "Actually we *did* have a fight. He got me a Christmas tree and I lost it."

"You lost the tree? How is that even possible?"

Hannah smiled. "No. I lost my temper. I thought Russell was ignoring my feelings in order to make himself happy. I said things I shouldn't have. Things I regret. So did he. I realize that he was right about a lot of things. I'd let my sister and former fiancé take something away from me that I love." She quickly summarized the events of the Christmas she discovered Gerald and Dinah together and her subsequent decision to avoid all things related to Christmas. "I'm not going to do that any longer. The past is the past and I'm over it. I can wait to tell him when he gets home. But I'd rather show him."

"I don't want to tell you what to do, but I'm going to anyway." Joni gestured at the Mrs. Claus costume. "Don't do this just for Russell. If you're happy ignoring Christmas and need to ignore it for a while longer, then do it. Do what is right for you. I'm sorry if I pressured you into participating in our Secret Santa gift exchanges and for all of the other Christmassy things I've roped you into doing over the years."

"Don't apologize. I actually had a good time. And I loved getting gifts and buying them for my friends. Who knows, maybe I've been slowly getting over the hurt without even knowing it. I certainly didn't feel bad when I saw Gerald. Apart from annoyance, I didn't feel a thing." She smiled as she realized the truth of those words. Gerald and his betrayal no longer mattered to her. She wasn't even angry at her mother and sister any longer. Nor was she still disappointed that she hadn't been able to rely on her only blood relatives. They were who they were. But she didn't wish them ill. She just wanted them to stay far away from her.

"I'm not doing this for Russell. I'm doing this for me. I want to embrace Christmas again. I want to enjoy what's left of this season and every one in the future."

"Are you sure?"

"I'm positive."

Joni smiled. "In that case I'll duck out so you can change. There's a rumor circulating that I'm going to be dressing up as Mrs. Claus. Some kids are worried that if I'm pretending to be Mrs. Claus that Santa Claus won't be real. When they see me and Mrs. Claus in the same room, that should put the rumor to bed. Plus, I'll be able to share the experience with Lex and Joshua."

It had never occurred to Hannah how much Joni and her family would enjoy sharing this moment together. She was even happier that she'd decided to be Mrs. Claus.

Joni zipped her boots. "Alyssa will come and get you once the kids are all settled. It should only be a few minutes. Then you'll stop and pick up Santa."

"Okay."

"Good luck."

"Thanks." Hannah quickly changed into the long red velvet dress with the white fake fur trim along the bottom, then put on the matching jacket and cinched the black belt around her waist. After pulling her hair into a thick braid, she put on the white wig. She took a quick look in the mirror and decided she made a pretty decent Mrs. Claus.

There was a knock on the door. "Are you ready?"

"Yep."

Alyssa opened the door and stepped inside. "So you're going to play Mrs. Claus instead of Joni. I bet Russell is going to love that."

"I hope so."

"We missed him at the boutique today. He's a lot of fun."

"He is," Hannah concurred. Her heart ached as

she recalled how they'd angrily pushed each other away. She just hoped he was as eager to see her as she was to see him. That would make things so much easier. "How do I look? Is my wig straight in the back?"

Alyssa gave Hannah a once-over, then tugged on one side of the wig. "All you need is the glasses and lace cap and you'll be fine."

Hannah donned the rest of the costume and Alyssa nodded with approval. "You're the best-looking Mrs. Santa I've seen. You're going to rock Russell's world."

"Thanks."

They closed Joni's office, then walked to the art room. As they went through the deserted halls, they could hear kids in the gym enthusiastically singing "Rudolph the Red-Nosed Reindeer."

"You and Santa are supposed to wait outside until they sing 'Santa Claus Is Coming to Town.'"

Hannah nodded. They'd reached the art room and she stood aside while Alyssa knocked on the door.

"Ho! Ho! Ho! Come on in."

Alyssa laughed and rolled her eyes, but she opened the door and leaned against it. "Come on, Santa. The kids are waiting for you."

"Is Joni with you?"

Hannah shook her head and pressed a finger to

her lips. Alyssa nodded and grinned. "Mrs. Claus is standing right outside the door. Come on."

Hannah heard footsteps and her heart began to pound as she anticipated seeing him again. And then there he was. Russell was dressed in the traditional Santa uniform. He'd obviously padded his middle and put on a long white beard that reached the middle of his roly-poly stomach. More white hair was visible beneath his red cap. Even wearing this costume, Russell still was the sexiest man that Hannah had ever laid eyes on.

She was watching him and knew the exact moment he realized that it was her standing there and not Joni. His eyes widened and then he smiled broadly. "Hello, Mrs. Claus." He leaned in closer and brushed his lips against her cheek. Her skin tingled and she felt some of the tension that had been squeezing her insides loosen. Though she'd been telling herself that things would work out between her and Russell, this was the first time that she truly believed it.

He held out his arm for her and she took it. "Ready to go, Mrs. Claus?" Russell asked.

"Absolutely, Mr. Claus."

Alyssa shook her head. "You guys are so corny. Follow me."

Hannah practically floated to the gym on Russell's arm. When they reached the door, Alyssa stepped inside and went to the front of the room.

She whispered something to Kenneth, who'd been leading the singing. He nodded and Alyssa went to sit with her family.

When the song ended, Kenneth spoke. "Our next song is 'Santa Claus Is Coming to Town.' Maybe if we sing it loud enough, he'll show up."

Several members of the high school band were providing accompaniment as the children sang at the top of their lungs. All in all it was pretty loud. Every Santa in the world probably heard them.

"That's our cue," Russell said. A large sack filled with wrapped packages had been placed outside the door. He picked it up and tossed it over his shoulder.

"I wish we had time to talk."

"We will. Later," Russell promised. "But for now, our audience awaits."

They stepped inside the gym and several kids screamed out "Santa!" Three of the younger ones broke away from their parents and raced over to them. Grinning, Russell stooped down and gave the three kids a hug before their mothers reached them and led them back to their chairs. Happiness bubbled inside Hannah and she laughed.

She felt the joy that had been missing from the holidays for years. It occurred to her that the joy she hadn't been able to find had been around her all the time. She'd only needed to look. It was in the excitement of the children, the affection shown from one friend to the other. The generosity of strangers. It was everywhere. Including inside her.

Waving to the children, she and Russell sat in the two large ornate chairs that had been placed on the makeshift stage. When the song ended, he stood and waved. "Ho! Ho! Ho! Merry Christmas, everyone."

"Merry Christmas, Santa!"

"And Mrs. Claus," a girl of about eight called out.

Hannah grinned. "Thank you. Merry Christmas to all of you."

"Have all of you been good?" Russell asked.

"Yes," the children roared.

He ad-libbed for a while, walking back and forth and talking to the children. He joked with a couple of the adults, musing aloud if they had been as good as they'd claimed.

Joni went to the microphone and announced that it was time for the kids to have a chance to meet with Santa, one on one. He sat back down as the kids formed a line along the gym wall. The younger ones squirmed with excitement, jostling each other.

As Mrs. Claus, Hannah didn't have a big role to play, so she sat and watched Russell. He was a marvel. The way he interacted with the children warmed her heart. He was so natural and comfortable with them, talking to each child and really listening to what they had to say.

Before each child sat down, one of the volunteers would get the child's name and search through the alphabetically arranged presents for the one chosen especially for him or her.

Hannah had stopped by one day when volunteers were wrapping the gifts. She'd been surprised to see some of the hottest toys of the season. She knew they'd raised funds, but there was no way they'd raised enough money to buy these toys. When Hannah had asked Joni about it, she'd only laughed. "My husband and sister-in-law are loaded. And fortunately, they're very generous. They matched our funds, making it possible for us to buy great gifts for everyone."

Even more evidence of Christmas spirit. How could she have missed it?

The line of kids moved fairly rapidly, but each child had the opportunity to talk with Santa for a minute or so. Every once in a while, a bighearted kid requested that Mrs. Claus be in the picture, too, so she wouldn't feel left out.

When the younger kids had finished, a few of the teenage boys approached Russell, joking about wanting to take a picture on Santa's lap. Russell laughed along with them.

"I wish I could," he said. "But Santa's not as young as he used to be. And the old body is kind of breaking down. But I'll gladly take pictures with you standing up."

The kids laughed and backed up. "I was just joking," the ringleader of the teens said.

"I thought your body was supposed to last forever. Isn't that what the story is?" another kid asked.

"Sadly, that's not true. It happens to the best of us. Even jolly old elves." Russell looked at the kids. "I've been watching you. I've seen you play basketball. You're good. All of you are."

"So were we naughty or nice?"

Russell stroked his long beard as if considering the question. "Well, I gotta tell you. I've seen the way you beat the older guys. You have no mercy on them. That's borderline naughty. But I've also seen the way you let the little kids win when you play against them, so it's a wash. Now let's take pictures and get your gifts."

They might have been teenagers, but they still liked getting presents. Naturally they hammed it up for the pictures so nobody would get the idea that they still believed in Santa at their ages.

Hannah stood on the sidelines, watching as Russell interacted with the teenagers. They were at that funny age, not quite kids but not quite adults, either. She couldn't hear all of the conversation, but she could tell that Russell was interested in what the kids were saying.

Russell put his arm around one of the teen's shoulders as the group walked to the table where the gifts had been stacked. In a few minutes, each of them was holding a box and smiling as they walked away.

Russell came over to Hannah. Even in his Santa suit, he had swagger. Some things just couldn't be disguised. He winked and her heart sped up. "According to the schedule, the party is going to end in about twenty minutes. Do you want to swing around and talk to the kids one more time before we head back to the North Pole?"

"Yes. That's a great idea." She would agree to just about anything if it included spending time with Russell.

They talked to several groups of kids who peppered Santa with questions about reindeer and elves, which he patiently answered. Joni approached them after a while and led them to the front of the room. Once she got the crowd's attention and everyone quieted down, she spoke. "It's time to say goodbye to Mr. and Mrs. Claus. Let's thank them for their presents."

"Bye, Santa," the kids called as Hannah and Russell left the party, waving and saying goodbye until they were out of the gym and out of sight of the kids.

"Let's get changed and meet out front," Russell said, as they neared the art room.

"Okay." Hannah left him there and returned to Joni's office to change. Her heart was pounding and her hands were trembling so much she could barely remove the costume. The moment of truth was growing near. After she'd put the dress and jacket back on the hanger, and placed the wig in its bag, she put on her own clothes. She combed her hair and retouched her makeup. When she was done, she grabbed her purse, stepped outside and closed the door behind her, then headed to the front entrance of the building.

She didn't know what Russell was going to say, but she knew her life would never be the same after this night.

Russell watched as Hannah approached him. Dressed in a blue dress that accentuated every curve on her sexy body, she was a vision, outshining the lights strung throughout the youth center. She smiled and the blood heated in his veins as his heart filled with joy. There was something about Hannah that made him happy. Just being around her made him believe that everything would work out. Despite everything she'd been through, there was a lightness to her. A natural joy.

He took her hand and they walked to their cars. He opened her door and watched as she drove away before getting into his car. The ride back to the house seemed to take twice as long as usual, but when he glanced at the clock, he realized it hadn't. That had been the anticipation talking.

He needed to get control of his feelings if he was going to be able to have a calm conversation. Russell parked his car and jumped out. She'd arrived before him and was standing outside her car. He closed the distance between them, and as they walked to the house, his eyes were drawn to the Christmas lights, which as usual were on.

He stopped and looked at her. "Why didn't you turn off the timer? I know you don't actually like the lights."

She smiled. "That's not entirely accurate."

"What do you mean?"

"I'll tell you once we get inside."

That comment built on the hope he'd felt when he'd seen her dressed as Mrs. Claus. She'd been adamant about not wanting to play the role at the party and had been upset when he'd mentioned it. Then he'd really messed up by giving her a Christmas tree. It had taken a while for him to get it through his head, but he'd finally accepted the fact that she didn't like Christmas and that she had no use for the outward displays like lights and trees.

And that was fine with him. She got to decide how and if she observed Christmas. He just wanted her to be happy.

They stepped inside and took off their coats.

"How about some hot cocoa and cookies?" he

asked. Although he was anxious to have this conversation, he wanted them to be comfortable while they talked.

"You want to eat?" Her voice rang with surprise.

"I had an early dinner and it's long gone."

She laughed. "To be honest, I didn't eat much today, either. What if I scrounge up some dinner while you get a fire started? How's that sound?"

That sounded promising to him. And better than he'd expected a few hours ago. "I can do that."

While he added wood and kindling to the fire, he heard her bustling around the kitchen. He'd moved the chairs from in front of the fireplace and was in the middle of setting pillows and cushions on the floor when she returned. She was carrying a tray with a steaming bowl, plate, and mug apiece. He dropped the pillows and rushed over to help her.

"Thanks." She gave him the tray and then sat on one of the cushions.

He joined her and they ate in silence for a few moments. When he'd formulated his speech, he looked in her eyes. They were so clear. So beautiful.

Summoning his courage, he inhaled and then spoke. "Hannah, I am sorry for the way I behaved. First, I'm sorry for buying you a tree. If I would have thought it through, I would have realized that it would bring you pain. I'm also sorry for the things I said. Your time is not my time. You have a right to deal with your feelings in your own way. Just as I did with mine."

She smiled and touched his hand. Despite the seriousness of the moment, electricity shot through his body. "Thank you. I appreciate the apology. And I want to apologize to you, too. I spoke harshly. Criticized you. I can't imagine what it would feel like to lose the career you've had since you were a teenager and planned to have much longer. But I know it must be heartbreaking. I'm sorry you're going through this."

He nodded. She'd understood how he'd felt without him going into great detail. "So where do we go from here?"

She didn't look at him at first, choosing instead to focus on the floral pattern on her mug. Then she looked him in his eyes. "Well, I'd like to continue our pretend relationship."

"About that."

"What?" She sounded leery. Was she afraid about what he would say? Didn't she know how he felt? He must have hurt her more deeply than he'd known.

"I was on my run today and went past the B&B."

"Did my mother or sister do something to offend you? I'm sorry."

"No. It was nothing like that. They didn't even see me, though I did see them."

"Okay. That's a relief. Then what?"

"They left town today. I guess they finally figured out that they weren't going to be able to convince you to design that dress for Dinah or introduce them to your rich friends."

"Wow. I knew they were planning on leaving in a couple of days. I guess that means we only need to keep on pretending to be in love for your parents."

He shook his head. "I had lunch with my parents today and told them everything."

She smiled, but it didn't look sincere. "Oh. I guess there's no reason for us to continue to pretend."

"No reason at all."

"So what does this mean?"

Hannah was looking down, pulling at a thread in her dress. He put his hand on hers, stilling it before she could pull it loose. "It means we don't have to pretend to be involved. It means, I would like to date you for real."

"What?"

"I want to date."

"Really?"

He realized he'd chickened out. He needed to put it all on the line and say what he truly meant. He might not be a soldier for much longer, but no longer wearing a uniform didn't turn him into a coward. He reached out and caressed her cheek.

Her skin was so soft. So warm. "Not just date. I want to keep our relationship going. I've enjoyed every moment we've spent together. I want to change our fake relationship into a real one. I want to see where things go. We can both be happy together. That's what I want. Now, what do you want?"

She smiled and leaned her face into his palm. "I want two things. First, I do want to continue our relationship. I started out pretending, but it didn't take long for my feelings to become real."

His heart skipped a beat even as he began to believe everything would work out. "I thought I was the only one whose feelings were changing. But I'd hoped you felt the same."

"You were right."

"My future is a bit up in the air right now. I earned degrees in counseling and child psychology and hope to put them to use. I might go into private practice or work in a school."

"That sounds good to me. I saw the way you were with those kids. You're a natural."

He had to admit he'd enjoyed interacting with the kids and could imagine doing more of that in the future. It would be a place to start. "You said two things. What's the second?"

She brushed her lips against his and then smiled. "I want to bring the tree back into the house and decorate it together."

"What? No. You don't have to do that. You don't have to prove anything to me."

"I know. And it's not about proving anything. You were right. I was letting one incident have too much impact on my life. Granted, it was a horrible incident, but still… If I don't want it to take control of my life, I need to let it go. I've always loved Christmas. I enjoyed it from the time I was a child. And I want to start enjoying it again. With you."

"I was going to talk to Lex about donating the tree to a needy family. Lucky for you, I didn't have time. It's in the backyard. So if you'll come with me, we can drag it inside."

She jumped to her feet. He stood, too. They put their coats back on and went out back and grabbed the tree. It was still in good shape. Once it was inside, they put it in the stand, then carried the bins of ornaments and lights into the front room. As he started to wrap a string of lights on the bottom, she stopped him.

"What?"

"We're missing something."

"What's that?"

"Music."

He used an app on his phone and found a station streaming Christmas songs. As the music filled the air, they began to sing along. When the tree was decorated, they stood back and admired it.

He wrapped his arms around her waist, and she leaned back against his chest. "Thank you."

"You're welcome." He kissed her cheek. "Merry Christmas."

"Merry Christmas."

* * * * *

Don't miss a single
Story in Kathy Douglass's
Sweet Briar Sweethearts series:

How to Win the Lawman's Heart
The Waitress's Secret
The Rancher and the City Girl
Winning Charlotte Back
The Rancher's Return
A Baby Between Friends
A Soldier Under Her Tree

Available from Harlequin Special Edition.

WE HOPE YOU ENJOYED
THIS BOOK FROM

HARLEQUIN
SPECIAL
EDITION

Believe in love. Overcome obstacles. Find happiness.

Relate to finding comfort and strength in the
support of loved ones and enjoy the journey
no matter what life throws your way.

6 NEW BOOKS AVAILABLE EVERY MONTH!

COMING NEXT MONTH FROM

⬦ HARLEQUIN
SPECIAL EDITION
Available December 29, 2020

#2809 HER TEXAS NEW YEAR'S WISH
The Fortunes of Texas: The Hotel Fortune • by Michelle Major
When Grace Williams topples from the balcony at the new Hotel Fortune, the last thing she expects is to find love with her new bosses' brother. Wiley Fortune has looks, money and charm to spare. But Grace's past makes her wary of investing her heart. This time, she is holding out for the real deal...

#2810 WHAT HAPPENS AT THE RANCH...
Twin Kings Ranch • by Christy Jeffries
All Secret Service agent Grayson Wyatt has to do is protect Tessa King, the VP's daughter, and stay low profile. But Tessa is guarding her own secret. And her attraction to the undercover cowboy breaks every protocol. With the media hot on a story, their taboo relationship could put everything Tessa and Grayson have fought for at risk...

#2811 THE CHILD WHO CHANGED THEM
The Parent Portal • by Tara Taylor Quinn
Dr. Greg Adams knows he can't have children. But when colleague Dr. Elaina Alexander announces she's pregnant with his miracle child, Greg finds his life turned upside down. But can the good doctor convince widow Elaina that their happiness lies within reach—and with each other?

#2812 THE MARINE MAKES AMENDS
The Camdens of Montana • by Victoria Pade
Micah Camden ruined Lexie Parker's life years ago, but now that she's back in Merritt to care for her grandmother—who was hurt due to Micah's negligence—she has no plans to forgive him. But Micah knows that he made mistakes back then and hopes to make amends with Lexie, if only so they can both move on from the past. Everyone says Micah's changed since joining the marines, but it's going to take more than someone's word to convince her...

#2813 SNOWBOUND WITH THE SHERIFF
Sutter Creek, Montana • by Laurel Greer
Stella Reid has been gone from Sutter Creek long enough and is determined to mend fences...but immediately comes face-to-face with the man who broke her heart: Sheriff Ryan Rafferty. But as she opens herself up bit by bit, can Stella find the happily-ever-after she was denied years ago—in his arms?

#2814 THE MARRIAGE MOMENT
Paradise Animal Clinic • by Katie Meyer
Deputy Jessica Santiago will let nothing—not even a surprise pregnancy—get in the way of her job. Determined to solve several problems at once—getting her hands on her inheritance *and* creating a family—Jessica convinces colleague Ryan Sullivan to partake in a marriage of convenience. But what's a deputy to do when love blooms?

HSECNM1220

"I didn't fall," she announced with a wide smile as he
returned the crutches.

"You did great." He looked at her with a huge smile.

"That was silly," she said as they started down the walk
toward his car. "Maneuvering down a few steps isn't a
big deal, but this is the farthest I've gone on my own
since the accident. If my parents had their way, they'd
encase me in Bubble Wrap for the rest of my life to make
sure I stayed safe."

"It's an understandable sentiment from people who
care about you."

"But not what I want."

He opened the car door for her, and she gave him the
crutches to stow in the back seat. The whole process

was slow and awkward. By the time Grace was buckled in next to Wiley, sweat dripped between her shoulder blades, and she felt like she'd run a marathon. How could less than a week of inactivity make her feel like such an invalid?

As if sensing her frustration, Wiley placed a gentle hand on her arm. "You've been through a lot, Grace. Your ankle and the cast are the biggest outward signs of the accident, but you fell from the second story."

She offered a wan smile. "I have the bruises to prove it."

"Give yourself a bit of…well, grace."

"I never thought of attorneys as naturally comforting people," she admitted. "But you're good at giving support."

"It's a hidden skill." He released her hand and pulled away from the curb. "We lawyers don't like to let anyone know about our human side. It ruins the reputation of being coldhearted, and then people aren't afraid of us."

"You're the opposite of scary."

"Where are we headed?" he asked when he got to the stop sign at the end of the block.

"The highway," she said without hesitation. "As much as I love Rambling Rose, I need a break. Let's get out of this town, Wiley."